CHAPERONING PARIS

COLLINS BROTHERS BOOK 1

VICTORIA PINDER

SOUL MATE PUBLISHING

New York

CHAPERONING PARIS

Copyright©2014

VICTORIA PINDER

Cover Design by Niina Cord

This book is a work of fiction. The names, characters, places, and incidents are the products of the author's imagination or are used fictitiously. Any resemblance to actual events, business establishments, locales, or persons, living or dead, is entirely coincidental.

All rights reserved. No part of this publication may be reproduced, stored in a retrieval system, or transmitted in any form or by any means (electronic, mechanical, photocopying, recording, or otherwise) without the prior written permission of both the copyright owner and the publisher. The only exception is brief quotations in printed reviews.

The scanning, uploading, and distribution of this book via the Internet or via any other means without the permission of the publisher is illegal and punishable by law. Please purchase only authorized electronic editions, and do not participate in or encourage electronic piracy of copyrighted materials.

Your support of the author's rights is appreciated.

Published in the United States of America by
Soul Mate Publishing
P.O. Box 24
Macedon, New York, 14502

ISBN: 978-1-61935--762-4

ebook ISBN: 978-1-61935-472-2

www.SoulMatePublishing.com

The publisher does not have any control over and does not assume any responsibility for author or third-party websites or their content.

To my Mom.

She might never read anything I write,

but if I need her for anything, she's there.

I have the best mom in the world.

She loves me and will do anything I ever need.

I was a bratty teenager, but, Mom, I love you.

And you're amazing,

good-natured about everything in my life,

and you need to believe in yourself, too.

You're better than you think.

Acknowledgements

I started this story when I still lived in my parents' house, in my pink room, studying for college. It was badly written then, but the idea was there. When I needed inspiration for something to write, I reread my own stuff, reconnected to the story and my awesome vacation to Paris I took with my best friend at the time, Christine. She hated Paris. I secretly loved it. I'd go back there anytime, but that was back when I had no living expenses other than my car.

Chapter 1

Payback time. Standing in his mother's kitchen, Sean Collins smiled as he hung up the phone.

He hovered at the phone for a moment, then charged along the carpeted hallway to his bedroom. In a flash, he changed from his T-shirt and jeans into his black pin stripe king-of-the-business-world suit complete with black tie and shiny black shoes.

Finished dressing, Sean jittered at the door and listened to his son talking nonstop to his mother upstairs. His skin tingled and he closed his eyes. At least moving to his parents' country estate where he had grown up on Cape Cod had been good for everyone.

Breakfast could wait. He grabbed the keys on the counter downstairs, and he called upstairs, "I'm leaving. I won't be gone long."

Last year, the school principal had fired him with bogus charges. Sean had sworn on every holy book that he'd been fired because his doctors had discovered cancer in a routine physical exam.

The sickness sucked. But he'd survived. And now he used his vast wealth to get what he wanted. No teacher should be treated so callously. He had taken the job at the time to prove to himself he had more choices than being the chief financial officer of his father's corporation.

He set his jaw and walked outside to his car, where the smell of freshly cut grass hit his senses.

The moment he stepped outside and headed toward the garage, Sean stared at the vast forested area on the property for a moment and pressed his lips together. Trees made sense. Women never had. His luck with women had been bad from the start. His first girlfriend, Gigi Dumont, had left him for parts unknown, and then later his wife, now his ex, Jennifer, had also left. She'd played with a whole set of loose scruples. But Jennifer hadn't hurt him, not like Gigi had. Sean rolled his shoulders. Why did everything in his life always seem to go back to Gigi leaving?

He fished out his keys from his pocket. And now Gigi had moved back into the house next door.

Sean opened the garage door. A quick click of a button and the gate lifted.

Last night he hadn't slept. Today his shoulders were straight. This moment had nothing to do with women and everything to do with justice. His fingers traced the shiny finish of his brother Gerard's Aston Martin. Without blinking, he opted to borrow the car. He'd be early and outshine everyone else. Gerard had offered to loan it to him specifically for today. Sean licked his lips and turned the key, igniting the engine, and took off.

A daydream flashed in his eyes. Principal Murray's jaw dropped to the ground in shock the second Sean stepped inside the office with the papers.

Sean clutched the wheel. He intended to twist the knife even further. People like Mr. Murray gave businessmen around the world the reputation of cold, heartless automatons, especially when he claimed the firing had been over "job performance." Every one of Sean's students had passed the state assessments.

Now, Sean ran the finances for his parents, his father's company, and his brothers. The support of his family to get him through cancer treatments had been phenomenal, but what if he hadn't had that support? What if he'd had no money to pay for treatments? He'd be dead because the principal had fired him due to the insurance increases. Well, now Sean had a better solution.

He sped down the country road for the half-hour trip. During his horrible marriage to Jennifer, he'd worked as a teacher, and his students had achieved both academic and social successes. Jennifer had been the nightmare that drove Sean away from Collins Industries, Collins Enterprises, Collins Investments, and Collins Mutual, to list a few of his father's multiple companies. Post divorce and cancer, Sean had made the decision to offer employees packages in cases of sickness. Anyone who worked for him would now receive a payoff equal to the job performance done over the years as part of a settlement. Money paid hospital bills.

Sean's stomach clenched as he gazed at the sign for the Barnstable Charter High School parking lot. Sean parked Gerard's fancy lawyer wheels that screamed "out to impress" right next to the about-to-be-sacked principal's BMW sedan. The Aston Martin made the perfect goodbye gesture. Murray had been outclassed.

Sean leaned forward in his seat, refusing to feel guilty. He waited for the school bell to ring and watched students bounding outside.

Unlike most people, his family had money, and normally he wouldn't like flaunting wealth. His Jeep Wrangler suited him just fine, but today he needed to look like the elite businessman he was. He stepped out a minute later, and in a fast walk, he strode down the halls. Sean winked the second he saw the school guard's shocked face.

"You had cancer?" asked the older African American lady who coached the wrestling team.

"Yes, I did. I'm better now," Sean said, smiling.

He inclined his head and passed the security desk then Sean turned right toward the principal's office.

In his briefcase he carried the school board's ruling and the proof of sale of the school to Collins Enterprises. Barnstable was a private school that followed school board law. The sale to his company had been finalized, but Sean had insisted on telling Murray in person. The minutes of the meeting would be posted at one that day. Victory waited for him, and justice tasted better than homemade chocolate chip cookies.

In the office, the overqualified secretary, Mattie, dropped her pencil on the floor. Sean made eye contact with her and the older woman smiled back. Then he picked up the pencil in stride, and handed it back to her. She opened her mouth to speak, and he shook his head, placing his finger over his lips to silently request her silence.

She smiled her response and swiveled her chair back to her computer.

He had seen Mattie in action and understood the older woman had known how to treat people more than anyone else in the office.

Outside the principal's door, Sean straightened his tie into perfect alignment. His heart rate sped up and his entire body became alert then he heard *her* voice.

Gigi, or should he say, Giovanna Dumont. Her quiet, sweet voice unmanned him, making his palms sweat. Why would she be here? And how could she still steal his breath away?

"Please, Murray, my students won the chance of a lifetime. We *earned* the school trip." Gigi argued her case with the principal in her sweet, honey voice. "If they win this competition, they are worldwide French Congressional winners. Two noble laureates named this year won this competition years ago, and we're one of three North American schools in the finals."

Murray never raised his face from his desk. He shrugged. "French is a dying language, Ms. Dumont. No one cares about the language, and my funding was reduced to the bone."

A wave of disbelief swept through Sean. Gigi taught here? Why? She didn't need a job, and she hated children. Wasn't that what she'd said years ago?

Gigi pleaded again, "Murray, this is so unfair."

Murray answered, "Life isn't fair."

Sean kept his head up and walked inside. *Guess I don't have a choice now.*

"Time to leave, Gigi," Sean said quietly.

Murray's black, beady eyes reminded Sean of a squirrel's. Gigi's mouth fell open. He'd deal with her after he dealt with the principal.

Sean leaned into the chair closer to her.

"Sean?" Gigi's eyes widened in shock. "What are you doing here?"

Lust rushed through his body. No. He would not be attracted to her again.

He stared at Murray, who didn't stand up. Sean refused to gaze at Gigi. Ignoring her had worked the past few months, and he saw no need to change strategies, even if her big blue eyes set him off.

"Please come back in a few minutes, Ms. Dumont," he said. "I need to speak to Murray alone."

"What did you call me? Ms. Dumont? First him, now you. Apparently, it's the meeting of the self-centered jerks."

Her words sparked with fire though the sharpness of each question hit him with her cutting accusations.

Gigi rolled her eyes. "Whatever. I'm leaving."

She huffed and sashayed her long skirt out the door.

Sean remembered staring at her sexy butt sway. But that was many, many years ago and he had always acted childish near her. *Damn*. Even now, her hips demanded his attention. He stopped staring the moment he could no longer see her.

Sean tugged his ear. Gigi Dumont was far too attractive to be a teacher.

At least he could forget Gigi for the moment. His eyes narrowed on his prey. Murray. Sean needed to see his face the split second he learned that the school board had revoked his license for illegal accounting at the school.

"Do you know why I'm back?" Sean asked Murray.

Murray shook his head, and then pushed his glasses up his nose. "Mr. Collins, there are no open faculty positions available at this school."

"I never needed a job from you." Sean dropped the papers on his desk. Murray could read either of them first. What mattered was standing up for others who might someday have to deal with cancer or another horrible life-threatening disease.

He stared as Murray read one then the other. A smile formed on Sean's face and he leaned on the desk. "Start packing your bags and go back to Boston where you belong."

"You can't do this!" Murray yelled.

"I can, and I will." Sean saw the surprise in the man's eyes, and the sharpened proverbial knife dropped hard. His righteous anger disappeared now as he witnessed Murray's forehead crumple. Sean had never been a bully, never liked kicking anyone when they were down, not even this despicable man. *Damn.*

"I bought the school. You're out."

"My hearing at the school board according to this paper is in two weeks . . ."

"Ten business days." Did the man intend to fight this? "It's a done deal."

Murray tugged at his collar for air. "While you signed the deeds of trust on my school, your ownership doesn't begin for another month."

Murray's argument had one valid point. But he refused to back down and wait for a month.

"Collins, why did you come after *me*?" Murray asked. "Why would a teaching position you never needed bother you enough to come back here?"

"I don't get to stare cancer in the eyes. It's silent and I had to depend on my strength. But I can stop someone like you from ever doing that to anyone else."

"What are you talking about?"

"Murray, you fired me when I told the office about my lung cancer caused from too much exposure to toxins while serving in the Marines." Sean plowed ahead, memories fueling his anger. "Not everyone has my options. You do not and can no longer fire people for being sick."

"Insurance—"

"Pack up this office, and I will decide what happens to this school." An image of Gigi floated back into Sean's mind eye. Damn. Blocking her from his thoughts was not working. "And to Ms. Dumont and her trip."

"I have two weeks?" The man's voice rose.

"To pack your bags, but you're done here. I make the decisions now."

"I'll start packing, but you'll see. The hearing *will* go my way," Murray argued. Had he not read the paper? "Since I'm in charge, Ms. Dumont's trip is cancelled for tomorrow."

Tomorrow? Sean's hands clutched together. "Prestige for academics is on my agenda." Not only that but Gigi's leaving the country would keep her away during the hearing. "Read who controls what. I'll be back. What room number is Ms. Dumont's classroom?"

"Fifty-seven."

Sean gazed back to see Murray slump in his chair to read the documents. Turning to leave the room, he asked one more question. "How long has Ms. Dumont been working here?"

"Since school began in September."

One month since she'd moved back into her mom's old home. The winter snow of February hadn't forced her to quit. She hadn't run off to Cabo San Lucas or wherever else her people took off to this time of year. From everything he'd heard about her, Gigi had lived a party after she ran away from her life in high school. Now she'd been working at the high school, teaching French for almost no money? *Why?*

Sean's steps echoed down the empty hallways. Today had been a half a day. He crossed his arms and stood outside Gigi's room. Sean needed a minute to catch his breath. He hadn't intended to ever knock at her door ever again.

His body tightened and he fixed his stare through the glass slit. He saw her sitting there grading papers. Years ago, Gigi had practically forced him to do his homework. For his entire childhood they'd cared about each other. They had shared their first kiss, their first everything.

He blinked but the memory of her lips lingered. Sean shook his head to block out the flashback. He stepped back and reminded himself to remember how she'd destroyed that version of herself by cruelly ripping his heart out at his birthday party.

Closing his palm over the classroom door handle, he pushed the door open.

Gigi stared up. The color drained from her face. She turned away and straightened her desk. Then she met his gaze and raised her chin. "You get to roam the halls here, Sean? Schools are secure buildings."

"I own this school now." No sense beating around the bush.

"You—" She stopped, then shook her head. "Why would you own a school? You hated learning when we were growing up."

"I could ask you the same thing. Why do you work here?"

A cough caught in her throat then she dropped her shoulders. "Am I fired?"

"Should you be?" His voice deepened as her nearness brought back memories.

Her lower jaw quivered. "I've changed the entire French programming. My students won awards unheard of in this state."

An uncomfortable silence stretched before them and his eyes never flinched. He studied Gigi. The earnest, wide-eyed woman that stared at him brought back images of the girl on the tire swings with pigtails in her hair, and the way she put stickers on his face. His childhood love for her had begun that day.

Now Gigi crossed her arms around her waist. "If I'm fired, I have a few things to pack up."

"You're not fired, Gigi." He took a step closer, and offered his hand to comfort her.

She brushed his hand and pushed back. An electrical spark bolted through him. Damn. After all these years she could still affect him that way. He stepped back, deliberately severing the connection. "Not unless you want to be. Have dinner with me tonight. Convince me about your trip to Paris."

"Dinner?" she asked. "You can't be serious."

"We can go to a local diner, nothing fancy. I don't want to keep you here longer than necessary. You can get me the details about the trip and give me time to make the arrangements afterwards?" He'd almost convinced himself. This would be a business dinner. Nothing more.

"Are you sure? Murray planned on canceling the trip to Paris."

Sean swallowed. "I'm not him, and you don't know me these days. I'm not the same man you knew, Gigi."

She closed her eyes. "All right. Give me a few minutes and tell me where. Driving with you leaves me stranded so I'd prefer to drive myself."

Why would she bring up that night now?

"You walked home on your own accord that night, Gigi. I followed you every step you took, offering you a ride."

"I know you did, Sean." She stared down, and wiped her eyes.

Was she crying? Then he heard her mumbling. What was she saying? He strained to hear her words. "You were hard, awful, and polite. Part of me never wanted to see you again."

"It's the same for me, but we have to move on. The past is behind us." Easy words, but could he?

She sniffled then raised her head. Her face was dry as she stared back at him. "Patrick okay?"

Last July, his son, Patrick, had ended up at Gigi's house because he'd been upset that his mother had died and his son feared his father might also die. Patrick was all he had left.

He hadn't known Gigi had returned to town until his mother had told him who'd found his missing boy. A war of emotions had run through him that day, and he had avoided Gigi ever since. He sighed then told her, "I never thanked you, and I should have."

"You tried when you showed up. I understood." She stood up to meet him. "We both have regrets, Sean. I'll meet you down the street at the diner. Give me ten minutes to pack up."

A clear message for him to leave now. He nodded. "Great. I look forward to hearing your plans for the trip."

He admitted to himself he looked forward to seeing her smile, too. So how did he make his heart stop pounding near Gigi Dumont?

Chapter 2

Gigi's neck stiffened but she finished tidying up her classroom, turned off the lights, and then left. What was she thinking? She would be eating dinner with the man who by all observable actions hated her for what she had done. She straightened her skirt with her palms. And she had no right to be attracted to him yet her legs were still weak from speaking to him a moment ago.

Once she made it to the office, she ran her hand through her hair and headed for the door. She would be late for her date with her past. Near the office sign-out sheet, she accidentally dropped her keys. She swooped down to pick them up when she saw Mattie waddle out, her arms piled high with papers and boxes. Mattie worked on attendance, wore a poker face at all times with the students, but she knew more about the school than anyone else.

"Ms. Dumont, can you help me carry a few things to my car?" Mattie asked.

"Of course."

Sean could wait a few minutes. How was it he ended up buying this school? He made zero sense.

Gigi took a brown box of papers from the woman's hands. "Are you parked in the faculty lot?"

"Yes, of course." Mattie's day must have been hectic. She brought a wheeled cart full of papers from the office and, trailing it behind her, she followed Gigi.

Gigi stared at the parking lot door, but fell back to walk beside the older lady.

Mattie smiled. "Quite a lot of commotion in the office today. Principal Murray getting fired and Mr. Collins returning from the dead then turning out to be the new owner. The whole office is in an uproar."

"Sean worked here before?" "You do know him then. I thought so from how he reacted when he saw you in Principal Murray's office."

Every hair on her arms and legs rose, and Gigi could swear she heard her heartbeat. "How did he react?" She'd been upset with Murray for threatening to cancel the Paris trip and hadn't paid much attention to Sean that moment.

"If you don't know, I ain't telling you." Maddie turned her face sideways and continued to gaze in his eyes. "Are you going to Paris tomorrow with your students?"

"I think so. I hope so." Sighing, Gigi opened the parking lot door, held it for Maddie, and stared up at the sky. "I'm going to meet Sean to beg for his approval. It's not my fault the law changed and Murray decided to cancel nonrefundable tickets and told me I need to tell parents tonight. He had no answers and offered no other solutions."

"That would cause every parent at the school to call in demanding someone's head on a platter."

"Yes, and guess whose head it'll be."

Mattie's eyes went wide. "Do you think Mr. Collins will find a solution other than firing you?"

"If he fires me, it wouldn't be because of the trip to Paris." Gigi couldn't meet Mattie's gaze. "He and I dated in high school. We broke up and never saw each other again. It's been easy to avoid him even if his family does live next door to me. We have our separate paths, different times we leave the house."

"Now he's the boss."

They walked through the corridor, out the door, and faced the afternoon sun.

"He's single. You're single. He's gorgeous, and he's under your skin. Go for it," Mattie encouraged.

"Sean Collins and I will never get back together." Gigi stared straight ahead, but felt the heat rise in her face. "I want to take my students to Paris. This is the reason we're eating together, nothing more."

"If you say so."

As they neared Mattie's car, Gigi's eyes gazed at Gerard Collins' fancy car as it passed out of the front gate. Shouldn't he have left already? Had Sean brought his brother to serve as backup to Murray? Gigi crossed her fingers. If there were two Collins at dinner tonight, then his brother would create a buffer between them. Her stomach tightened. Sean couldn't bring up the past if Gerard was there. Tonight the trip mattered, not her and Sean's broken hearts.

Gigi finished packing the boxes in Mattie's backseat then reached for the wheeled bag.

"Thanks, dear. I might not know the Collins, but you do. Please put in a good word for me and the rest of us at school. Nerves are going to be on edge in the coming weeks during this change of ownership. And in the middle of the third quarter in the school year," Mattie said, shaking her head.

Gigi closed the backseat door for her without saying a word.

"Mr. Murray never ran the place right," Mattie continued, "and Mr. Collins has a reputation for business and being a good teacher."

Why had Mr.-Richer-than-the-rest-of-the-world-population ever worked in a school setting? Sean preferred math, not people. She kept her opinion to herself. "Sean's fair-minded. I can't imagine him pushing any good people out. Read *Fortune 500* tonight. Six months ago there was a story about his health and—"

Mattie put her hand on Gigi's arm. "Stop procrastinating. Have fun on your date, dear. You're a good egg."

"Thanks, but it's not a date," Gigi reminded her.

"Sure, dearie. And one you're late for." Mattie opened her car door on the driver's side. "You might want to put on lipstick before you see him."

Gigi nodded to Mattie then hurried to her car. Once inside, she practiced her breathing techniques to release the tension in her body. Her therapist had ordered her to stay calm. He'd also said to forgive herself. Her body flashed hot. Sean would never forgive her for what she'd done.

Now for the sake of her students and her reputation as a groundbreaking teacher, she had to face him. *Deep breath in, long exhale out*. Burying her mother hadn't been this soul-stealing.

Gigi stared as Mattie's car went through the gates, then started her car. Time to face the music, however discordant.

A few minutes later, Gigi found a spot near the local small-town diner. Her eyes darted around and she spotted the sleek silver Aston Martin again. She rolled her shoulders. It might be easier to face the Collins clan, admit her sins, get the trip to Paris figured out, then make it home to catch up on her saved television shows for the week and relax.

Her stretch reminded her that her body still burned. Sean's brief touch earlier had left her simmering. She held her pocketbook closer to her body. He'd not touch her again.

Gigi's chin lowered to her neck. To stop dwelling on the past, she reached into the backseat and felt around for her emergency heels and slipped them on.

At least she'd walk like a lady. She had given up any chance of happy-ever-after with Sean at age seventeen. In her panic, she'd broken up with him then taken off to San Francisco, then New York, then Amsterdam, and finally had settled down in Paris, all before her eighteenth birthday. Ten years hadn't taken the pain away.

Finally, she stepped out of the care and headed for the door.

The bell dinged above her head and she gazed around. Her eyes stared at Sean sitting in a booth. Alone. Memories came flooding back of the many times they had snuck out of their high school to grab breakfast in a similar place. How they'd giggled and laughed, fully entrenched in the feelings of young love. Sean had been cute in high school. She licked her lips and stared. The years had enriched his appearance, transforming him from cute to drop-dead gorgeous. No one in the place could hold a candle to him.

She lowered her hands down her side, took one long, soothing breath, then she marched to the executioner's chair. Without a glance at him, she plopped down, and picked up the menu.

He stood to greet her then sat back down. She stared at her menu, ignoring his chivalry.

He cleared his throat. "Gigi, you surprised me today."

"Ditto that, baby." A wave of heat flashed to her face. Did she just call him 'baby'? What was wrong with her? He wasn't her baby anymore, and she wasn't a teenage girl.

His smirk hadn't changed. "Baby? That's how you're going to greet me?"

She ignored his comment and said, "Sean Collins, about the trip to Paris . . ." *Good. Focus on work.* "Do you know the whole situation?"

"No." He pushed her menu down.

Her face wrinkled but she did her best to continue avoiding eye contact.

Challenged, he tipped the menu completely back down to the table, and she hesitated another moment. She swallowed then braced herself to meet his stormy gaze.

Her face froze. His smile was friendly.

"What I know is Murray said no. Now tell me what's going on so I can help."

Her heart pounded against her chest. "Murray said yes originally. Everything had been approved. Then three days ago, school laws changed. There must be a female chaperone accompanying any female students, and a male chaperone with any male students. I'm a female—"

"Obviously," Sean said, his blue eyes twinkling. "And a pretty one."

"A flu wiped out the men." Heat rushed to her face, and she felt herself blush again, but continued. "Our plan was to travel to Paris. We have ten students in the group, six girls and four boys. So we need a male chaperone. Everything has already been paid for. We need someone fast, someone already approved in the statewide database, and Murray didn't want to brainstorm how to fix this snafu. His list of men didn't pan out and he didn't care. Five minutes before you walked in this morning, he ordered me to cancel the whole trip."

"Jeez. Are you serious, Scout? I mean, Gigi."

Scout? Her eyes widened and she stared at him. His did too. At least they both had memories to ward off. She'd once followed him to Cub Scouts to know what the boys did, and the nickname stuck. "He wanted me to call each student's parents and tell them they are out thousands of dollars for the plane tickets they bought for their son or daughter, not to mention the other things we'll be doing on the trip."

"You have to leave *tomorrow*?" Sean's eyes narrowed.

Gigi remembered that look. He'd squint his eyes then looked up to the left whenever he calculated math.

Her body went rigid and she continued. "Yes. We're to be in Paris for a week. We are the only East Coast school in the country eligible to go. It's not fair to the students who worked their butts off to make money." She slammed the tabletop for emphasis.

The waitress came over, studied them for a moment then as if having determined that everything was okay, she took the pencil out from behind her ear and asked, "Can I get your order, lovebirds?"

Sean's eyes darkened.

Long breath in, then out slowly. Gigi picked up the menu. "I'll have the chicken Caesar salad with the dressing on the side and water."

Pushing his menu forward toward the waitress, Sean smiled at her. "Large meat pizza and a pitcher of diet soda, two cups."

He couldn't be serious. Didn't he survive cancer? "Sean, that's not healthy."

"Thanks." He shook his head at the waitress then jerked his head toward to her. "She'll eat my food. She's skinnier than she should be. Bring fries, too."

The waitress chuckled then left.

"I need an inside scoop on what else Murray did. I'll solve the issue, and you can go tomorrow," Sean said, leaning forward.

"Thanks. I can't tell you how much I appreciate this. Ah, is Gerard here?" Her gaze darted around the small restaurant.

"My brother, no. Why?"

"That's his fancy car outside, isn't it? Unless your blue blood caught up to you today. I wondered if you had your lawyer sitting around waiting to pounce on me."

"After we eat, we can dig out the fighting sticks."

Gratitude should have showed up in her movement, but she couldn't find it. Gigi bit her lower lip. "Why are you being so nice to me?"

His audible sigh of relief relaxed her. "I'm alive, Gigi. Despite Jennifer. Despite the disease. I'm here. This makes you my last enemy to vanquish."

Vanquish? She knew it. "Just fire me. Don't tease me. Don't pretend to be nice and help me solve my problems. And don't call me Scout. Tell me how you hate me and get this over with."

"I was joking." He coughed. "I'm not over what happened between us. I'll never be, but I don't hate you. I never could." His voice sounded calm.

Her heart raced a mile a minute, and he had no idea.

"Tell me why you work at the school."

She sat up straighter, flexing her fingers. He had no clue who she was now. "I'm not rich, not like you, Sean. I've worked all my life, and I have certain restrictions on my life right now. That's pretty much it. Why did you buy the school?"

"Moral grounds? Did your inheritance not keep up with your fast lifestyle, Geegs?"

"I was young, angry, and rebellious." She knew better than anyone how she'd wasted so much of her life fighting, and, despite what Sean thought, she hadn't much money these days. "But that doesn't explain why Mr. Moneybags bought a school."

"Murray fired me when I was diagnosed with cancer. No one should be fired because of a disease. Gerard recommended a lawsuit, but I wanted swifter justice."

"Ahh." If Murray had done that, and she knew in her heart he had, then he deserved what Sean had done to him. "I hadn't known." The waitress brought their drinks and left. Gigi sipped her water. "Since we're being honest with each other about work, why did you want to work in a school? You love accounting and math."

"You're right. I have my reasons."

"Guess we're not sharing the important details, after all." Energy drained from her body, though she knew to keep her guard up.

"What do I need to do or say to get you to quit after your trip?" Sean asked, as he placed his hand on top of hers.

"You *are* firing me?" Closing her eyes, Gigi tried to focus. She needed the job. She had no other options, and this wouldn't be a problem if he hadn't bought the school. She breathed in and admitted she might have gotten fired over the Paris trip fiasco. "I've already prepared lesson plans for while I'm gone for the other students that aren't going."

"You're jumping to conclusions," he told her, removing his hand.

She shook her head, "You said you were going to convince me to quit."

"You don't need a job."

She crossed her arms, "Yes I do."

The pupils in his eyes grew larger. "I didn't say anything about firing you. I just want to know why you are there. You led the party-girl life last time I checked, not that you left much of a trail to follow unless you count your mother and her many pictures."

"She passed away. And I need my job." Her voice flatlined. Her mother had never treated her in a loving fashion. *She can't hurt me anymore.* But she kept that to herself.

"You inherited your mother's estate yet you work at a school? Help me understand."

"Why?" Her fingers itched to take his hand and the comfort he offered. But she wasn't insane. She held her arm on her lap, locking her other arm in. Sean's arms had held her for so much of her life, *before* she had grown up.

"We used to share everything."

Her vision turned blurry, and she couldn't focus. Her mother had made her lose everything. "Mom and I never talked. I don't know what she told you, but our version of events typically never matched." She could admit that much. She didn't want to go back to those memories. Guilt and pain would ratchet up and she'd end up curled up in a corner of the bathtub.

"I know you weren't close to your mother, and you shouldn't have been." He sighed. "She stood in our way once."

"How would you know that?" Startled by his revelation, she looked into his eyes.

"We dated for a long time, Gigi. Our entire childhood, at the times when most children don't know what the other gender looks like. Or feels like." His voice lowered. "*I know you*. You didn't make that choice."

"I try not to think about the past. I get too upset." Part of Gigi, the part that hadn't taken responsibility for her own decision, blamed both Sean and her mother. For years on the run, she numbed the pain with alcohol and parties. As an adult, she could now admit that Sean hadn't done anything wrong. *She* had. "You're right. Mom and I weren't close. She didn't want me to inherit a dime, but she didn't want to look bad to her friends by cutting me off. The pain she caused me only ever empowered her to be more hurtful. Now I'm following her dictates from the grave."

"You were always sensitive. Part of what made you special was how you expressed everything. The reason why you are living next door again?" He blinked.

Was that a question? She nodded. "Mom's will had certain *demands,* shall we say."

"I see." Light dawned in his eyes. "You're working to meet a condition of her will to get your hands on her money. How long do you have to stay, Gigi?"

"It's not the will, exactly." He didn't have to sound excited. Sean hadn't been part of the plan. Seeing him brought back all the pain she needed to push away. What she'd done all those years ago brought another wave of guilt crashing onto her shoulders. "It's the money. I have to work a year."

His eyebrow quirked. "What were you going to say before that?"

"Umm, I was deciding what Nicole Wyman movie I wanted to watch tonight." She hadn't covered her evasion well. He cocked his head and she knew he didn't believe here.

"Yeah right. Gigi, your mother—"

"Stop." She sliced the air with her hand to silence him. He did know her well. How did he push past her defenses like this, even after all these years? "I spent most of my adult life hating her. In fulfilling her wishes. I want to move on. I want a different life."

The food came out, and their discussion stopped.

Sean cut a slice of pizza, placed it on a plate, and slid it next to her salad. Then he served himself. The waitress left.

"I can't eat this," Gigi said and turned her nose up in the air.

"You're skinnier than I remember you, and food keeps the spirit strong. There is something making you afraid."

Dang. Coldness dug deeper into her body. She diverted and changed topics. "How are you doing, Sean? I heard about your cancer before today, and your wife dying."

"Jennifer left me before she died," Sean said, before gobbling his entire slice of pizza. "Her dying saved Gerard legal work."

"Sean, that's cold." Her fork swirled in her salad. Did he even care about his wife? She couldn't ask that question, though. Way too personal. "You're not hard or mean. Or have you changed?"

"I'm not your project anymore. We all grow up. Let's talk about something else."

Where had that come from? Had she hit a nerve? Hurting him had never and would never be in her plans. High school memories drifted back with every sip of her soda. She pushed her uneaten salad to the side. Soon, she'd remember the pain. "How do you enjoy living on the Collins compound again?" she asked, deliberately changing the subject.

"Our property is good for me, though a bit small. I want to find a place near home. Selling your home soon, Gigi?"

Small? The man's family could fit the entire village inside that house and still have room for royal guests to arrive.

"No. Why sell? I have rich neighbors who keep driving up the value." She'd worked hard to clean the cobwebs of her fights with her mother out of the house, and now she needed to exorcise the memories of Sean Collins from her mind. Facing what she'd thrown away might be therapeutic. "I don't know what the future holds for me, but for now, I need to be in my house."

She ate the pizza in silence.

"I heard a lot of bad things about you after you left, from crashing cars to partying until all hours of the morning," Sean asked.

"From my mother?"

Sean's color on his cheeks rose. "Yeah."

Why hadn't anything she'd ever done be good enough? She'd never had anyone but Sean in her corner growing up. "I wasn't even eighteen then and on my own for the first time." She paused. "I've faced my demons since then, Sean, but for that year of my life, after I left here, I didn't care what happened to me. Part of me wanted to die, but overcoming the depression matured me."

She sat up straighter and ate one of Sean's fries. "I'm sitting here asking you for help when you have every right to despise me for what I did." She gave a small smile, despite the ache in her body. "The fact I led my students to winning Nationals and the preliminary international rounds of the competition . . . I'm giving back now. This is *my* time."

"Good. And for the record, I never trusted your mother anyhow."

"Good." She trailed her fingers along her upper chest with the intent of clutching her necklace, but she forcefully dropped her hand. She tensed her jaw then set about acting like he already agreed with her. She stared down at the table to her uneaten salad. "Sean, thank you for finding a male chaperone for this. My students will appreciate it."

"I said that?" He winked at her. Did the man never get flustered? But she raised her eyebrows in a dare. He smiled back. "Well, then I never fail when I give my word. You'll go on the trip tomorrow."

"Thank you again." Trusting him came easy, and she shouldn't be catty. Unlike her, Sean had always kept his word.

He ate another slice of pizza and pushed another piece at her. His square chin had become more defined with age. Once, a lifetime ago, his lips had made hers quiver.

He slowly finished chewing, then added, "I'll need a list from you of the students, the parents, and the itinerary."

"Sure. No problem." Her spirits lifted. She *could* sit next to Sean, without falling apart. She watched as he wrote down something on a napkin then dug into the pizza.

Now that she could relax some, she realized that the pizza tasted delicious. Spicy sausage, pepperoni, and gooey cheese. It had been a long time since she'd had a treat like this. Without asking, she finished her slice, and he handed her the napkin. He'd written his email address on it.

"Thanks," she said. "I'll send you the list when I get home."

"What time's the flight?" He sipped his soda.

Shuddering, she remembered that pesky detail. "We have to be there at four A.M."

"Look for me at the airport. I'll make sure all the details are handled."

Sean finished the last slice. No more words were necessary. Her heart had never doubted he'd help her. He reached for her hand, but she pulled back. "I won't bother you anymore."

"Gigi, wait."

The 'but' she feared would surface now. She closed her eyes and pictured the executioner's final swing at her neck. To stop the daydream, she opened her eyes and met his serious gaze. "Yes?"

"You were right. I did want to fire you. But that was just a childish impulse." He wiped his hand with a paper towel and stared at her. "Now I don't know what to do about you. I've never forgotten what happened with us. I count you as an important part of my past, a life lesson." He cleared his throat. "Now you're back. The Paris situation is temporary, and for the benefit of the students and their parents, don't stress this. I'll see that the trip goes smoothly."

Gigi slumped forward, feeling some of the tension easing from her body. No 'but.' Sean had never hurt her. She had hurt him. She paused, then answered, "Sean, I can't thank you enough. Good night."

Rushing out of the restaurant, Gigi refused to look back. Trusting Sean came as natural to her as breathing. Sometimes difficult, but more often than not easy and natural.

Her feet pounded on the cement as she opened her car door. She wouldn't be able to make up for what she'd done all those years ago hurt. She'd had ruined them.

Sean Collins was the biggest regret she had in life but he had a life of his own now. He'd been through too much, and her demons were her own to battle through.

Once upon a time, though, she'd have given anything for him.

Chapter 3

A loud fire engine siren startled Gigi, sending her heart beat pounding against her chest. She rubbed the sleep from her eyes, then she opened them to see the glaring blinking red numbers. 3 AM. Time to get up. Her body stiffened, but she sat up. Groaning, she stretched, but even that didn't help her focus. Her thoughts focused on her one salvation. Coffee.

Her movements were slow but she forced her tired body to move. She stumbled a bit, but she dressed. Glancing at the clock again, she stared in disbelief. How? She'd lost fifteen minutes.

Drat. Her limbs refused to function, and her mind reeled. She needed some caffeine. Now. But no coffee shop opened at the early morning hour, and she had no coffee in the refrigerator. She'd meant to pick some up yesterday after work but ended up meeting Sean instead. She glanced down at her clothes, her black travel pants and a plain white blouse. Somehow, she'd make do. She grabbed her suitcase then left the house.

Next thing she realized, she stared ahead of her and made it to the highway.

In ten minutes, she'd be to the airport. On time for this trip to Paris. Away from Sean. Good. She'd recoup her energy there.

Airports had coffee vendors.

A smile formed on her face.

Then her car engine wheezed.

What? That sound couldn't be good.

The wheel and her car jerked to a stop. Ughh. Getting to this flight had to happen. Too many people depended on her. Sniffling from the cold air, she laid her head against the steering wheel and thought about giving up. Who could she call at this hour? It wasn't like she had any family, and the one she'd been born into would have preferred she'd roll over in her grave.

With a sigh, Gigi refused to give up. She clutched her cell phone, intending to call Sean. She almost dialed, but then saw headlights behind her.

What now? Someone going to kill her, or help her? She laughed off her overactive mind. Then she stared over her shoulder, and she saw a man in a business suit getting out of his truck. He approached, lowered his head to her open window, and asked, "You having trouble?"

"My car died. I need to get to the airport."

"Let me have a look," he said. "I used to be a mechanic. Where are you flying off to this early in the morning?"

"Barnstable Municipal airport to catch the first flight to Boston." She smiled. "It's the class field trip."

The man kept his hands on his sides until he fingered the hood of her car. She called out, "What can I do to help?"

"Stay inside, ma'am. Hit the release."

She popped the hood, and he disappeared behind it. What would she do if he didn't fix this? Call Sean? How had her life spun so fast in this new direction?

Two minutes later, her car sparked back to life.

She sighed and stretched.

The man slammed the hood and walked around to her window, wiping his hands on a handkerchief. "Just a loose wire. You're all set now."

Gigi smiled, and she waved at him and tipped her head back. "Thank you so much."

"No problem. Have a great trip." The man turned and headed back to his car.

She should repay him. She quickly reached for her purse, but she knocked it onto the floor. She grabbed some money and opened her door to chase him with the offer, but he'd already turned his truck back on the road. Her chest expanded. People helped each other here.

She had missed that.

She slammed on the gas pedal and raced to the airport. Speed helped make up lost time, and at this hour no one was on the road. She angled into a parking spot then ran inside the airport with her bag.

Getting through security seemed to take forever. Chaperones were supposed to be first to arrive, not the last. Her heart pounded with every step. She cleared the gate then spotted her students sitting together, seemingly unconcerned. Sucking in her breath, her eyes focused on a muscular forearm holding a cell phone to his ear.

Sean Collins!

Her heart fell to the floor. She lost track of her body and all she could do was stare in shock. No other man stood nearby.

Sean hung up the phone, winked at her, then announced, "Ms. Dumont is here. Let's board."

The students waved at her. Sean laughed at something, and her right foot to twitch. Her fingers wiggled then she took in a deep breath of air.

"Gigi, Miss Dumont, come on. We're behind schedule."

With effort she continued to go one foot in front of the other foot, but her legs became heavier. Walking took every ounce of willpower she had. Sean? Going? No. He was probably there to assure everybody got off all right. She closed the distance between them and said, "Sean, what are you doing here?" Then she knew. He couldn't get through security without a boarding pass. Maybe he had a business trip?

"My parents will watch Patrick for the week. I told them I needed to go somewhere for work, and that I'll bring them back something from Paris."

"Patrick lost his mother. Your going away can't be good for him." She paused, wracking her brain. "Besides, your father is likely working late hours and your mother is getting up there in years."

"He is fine. Mom was excited." He ignored her concern. "Besides, if I don't go, then your students don't get to compete. I'm fingerprinted and available. Plus, I own the school, without anything else pressing to do at the moment except make sure this trip goes off without a hitch. So, let's go."

Gigi swallowed and turned toward the students, all gathered in groups and chatting excitedly. She should have been prepared for this possibility. She'd just trusted that Sean Collins kept his word, always.

Closing her eyes, she had to give up her plan to avoid Sean now. He'd stay in the same hotel. She'd see him everywhere she went. Opening her eyes, she realized she had fallen behind and ran to catch up.

Her eyes gazed at the numbers then stared at her phone. Her flight had been changed. She crossed her arms and asked, "Why are we in the terminal for private airplanes?"

Sean slowed down to get in step with her. "I called the parents last night. I got verbal permission last night then hand-collected a permission slip from every parent approving the change in flights."

"The Collins jet is *not* okay, Sean." She stopped mid-stride. "I don't take private jets."

"Why?"

"You wouldn't understand."

Sean gently touched her shoulder to get her to move, but she stepped away from him. Her arms waved in front of her and she shook. "Don't. I'll take my original flight and meet you there."

"The law states chaperones of *both* genders. Get on the plane."

Fear fluttered in her heart and tears swelled in her eyes. "Please. Don't."

Sean would think her crazy. She took a trembling breath and added, "Six years ago I took an offered ride from Prince Roberto. Our flight crashed. I thought I'd die. But I never had a scratch, and for six long hours, I nursed Roberto and his pilot to keep them alive. I swore to never trust a private plane."

"I'd make sure you're safe." His hand brushed her arm, and her arm had electrical currents rushing through her. He whispered, "You know you can trust me. Remember?"

Sean wouldn't hurt her physically, but he'd break her heart, if she let him in again. "You don't talk like you hate me. You should. I need the buffer."

"Gigi." Sean put his hand on her shoulder again, and she moved in step with him. "Holding on to the past isn't healthy. Let things go."

"Says the man who bought a school because he didn't like the principal."

"I had my reasons." He sighed. "You're right, but unlike you, I don't hide from the action."

Could he stop knowing her so well? "I don't hide."

"You don't live. You don't leave your house." He kept his grip firm and kept their pace fast.

"How do you know?" Did he spy on her? Avoiding his eyes, she inspected the carpet.

"I know your neighbors."

"Stalkers. The whole family." She stared at the smiling faces of her students, excited to get on the private jet.

Sean nodded at the agent but kept his arm around Gigi, insisting she get onto the ramp.

The teenagers flooded down the air the second they were signaled.

Gigi swallowed. She'd be strong for them. She wouldn't do this otherwise. "You can take your hand back."

"You are getting on the plane?"

"Yes. You're right. I can trust you."

The hum of the engines under her feet the second she stepped onto the flight brought back memories of the heat of fire about to consume her. Breathing deeply, she stared at Erica. Erica's parents had scraped together the airfare, and Gigi had collected some money from her teachers at school to ensure the girl could afford Paris.

Gigi watched as Erica smiled and laughed with her friend, buckling up without a care in the world. For Erica's sake and that of the other students, Gigi propelled herself forward till she sank into her seat.

Sean spoke to the pilot, and images flashed through her mind of her fighting off the un-noble royal. The jerk then stalked off to confide with his pilot moments before the plane crashed into a mountain. Sean's help then would have been nice.

No. She would not think of the crash right now. Sean, she'd think of him. His name burned into her mind and vibrated in her body. He had been her best friend, first and best lover, and as far as she knew had never hurt anyone. The years might have hardened him, or maybe she had, but she trusted him. His lips tasted better than any French wine. Her gaze found his broad, strong back and she let her shoulders relax. He'd never let anyone hurt them. He'd keep them safe. Sean finished his conversation then turned in her direction. Her eyes met his stormy blue ones, and his lips curled the same way she remembered.

Memories slammed into her and she averted her gaze as heat rose in her body. She had destroyed them both. She had no rights to count on his strength.

A hand on her arm forced her to look up. Her racing heart grew faster on contact. Sean. He squatted next to her to whisper in her ear, "Everything will be fine."

The concern in his voice captured her attention. She stared at his lips and another memory flashed. His hard lips had softened the moment he'd brushed against hers. Dropping her eyes, she hoped the heat in her face didn't create a blush as she told him, "Thanks."

"Just looking out for you." He handed her a blanket and pillow.

She accepted them and tried to still her rising pulse. Sean shouldn't care about her. She had no right to ask him for anything.

A week with Sean in Paris loomed ahead of her. Her eyes darted around the room. Her heart beat in her ears so loud, she drowned out the sound of the engines.

Chapter 4

"Please keep your seats in the upright position for landing."

The plane landed safely at Le Bourget Airport, the closest private plane airport near Paris.

Sean kept his gaze on the students and closed his file as the plane's tires bounced on the tarmac. Everyone stayed calm in their seats. Good.

His gaze wandered back to Gigi. With her eyes closed, Sean Collins couldn't see her brown eyes. Her light brown hair with curls at the ends hadn't changed. He could still close his eyes, and remember her berry smell of that hair the moment he'd first kissed her.

But at his birthday party, she'd marched in and told him what she had done. She had shook her head and walked out of his life.

Sean turned back in his seat.

Once the plane stopped at the terminal, Sean stood and stretched. He gazed at Gigi who suddenly rushed to the bathroom. One of the students, Kendra, the cheerleader, whispered to the boy student, David, "I can't wait to see the Eiffel Tower. It's like my dream."

Erica, the more studious girl, whispered to another female student, "Ms. Dumont and Mr. Collins took us to Paris to *win*, not for us to go to a on a vacation."

"We can do both." Sean answered, but his stomach clenched. Sean sucked his cheeks inside and turned away so the teenagers could not see him and counted to ten. *One. Two. Three. She hated him. Four. Five. Gigi lived a party.*

Six. Seven. She should not be a teacher. Eight. Nine. He didn't know what he wanted. Ten. Sucker. He breathed then turned to the students. "Let's go collect our bags and carry them to the private bus. I'll get Ms. Dumont."

The students gathered their belongings. Sean watched and waited. She stayed in. So he banged on the bathroom door, tapping his fingers after. "Gigi, do you need help? We're supposed to be watching your students."

"One minute."

She moved swiftly in the bathroom. He could hear the sounds of running water, sounding innocent. *Liar*. His lips flattened when she fell out of the small room. "Do you need me to get anything for you?" He offered, hoping he'd force the tension on his back to roll off.

"I'm good." She reached for her carry-on bag stored in the overhead compartment but he grabbed it before she could.

"Let me." Sean's body tightened. He needed to storm away from everyone and go get the car.

"Sean, I can carry my own things. I don't need your help."

He dropped her bag. "I was trying to be helpful."

"I can take care of myself." She had her hand on her hips. "Just leave me alone."

"With pleasure." A rock fell into his stomach.

She stormed off to lead the children off the ramp. He lost sight of her for the moment. His ex-wife hadn't hurt him, not like Gigi had. Gigi had left him bitter and cold. He followed behind the group and his gaze found her. Her swaying hips made him want to grab her and her eyes . . . Why did her eyes haunt him? He needed to let her go.

Sean sighed, ran his hand through his hair, and he focused on his goals. She hadn't wanted him. Not now and not then. This week he'd find a way to get over her. Seeing her again meant staring at the death of his own innocence.

Outside, he hailed a jumbo limo and called out to the group, "This way."

The children all stopped in their tracks and a limo door opened for Sean and the group. He waited for everyone to pile inside.

She wiggled past him. She still smelled of berries. He took a deep whiff. Then he rolled his back. Giovanna Dumont did not factor into his future. She represented the past.

Chapter 5

The chauffeured limousine kept the group in close quarters. Gigi's eyes narrowed in on Kendra and David. She noted how close they sat together, and the way his hand brushed hers. When had they begun dating?

Her gaze drifted, encompassing all her students.

"Buckle up, everyone," Sean said, and stuck his head into the door. "It's about ten miles between us and the Eiffel Tower near where our hotel is located."

"Miles or kilometers?" Erica asked.

Winking with an easy grin, he replied, "Miles. I calculate based on what I know."

"The European system makes more math sense."

"I'm American, though." Sean stared at Gigi for a minute and squeezed into the too-small group. "And last time I checked the passports of this group, everyone here is, too."

Gigi craned her neck, stared out the window, and frowned. She had booked a cheap hotel in Chinatown.

"We should have taken the bus I set up. We'll seem out of place." Sean must have read her blank look while she reached for her necklace. "I changed our hotel reservation to one of my family operations. It's five star and the entire staff will report any movements out of teenage rooms. This way we don't have to take turns staying up at night. My people will see."

Moans came from the teenage voices. Gigi schooled her emotion the best she could. She'd never played poker for a reason. "We'll talk when we get to the hotel, Sean."

He inched closer and whispered, "It wasn't for you."

"I didn't think so." Gigi fixed her stare straight out the window. She'd never tell Sean how often she dreamt of him. In the daylight it was easier to lose herself in the daily routine, not thinking. If she stared at him now, she'd see how she'd almost had everything.

He wrinkled his nose. She saw his reflection in the mirror as he told her, "It's to see that my investment at the school has credentials favoring Collins Enterprises."

"You don't have to explain to me, Sean." She squeezed his arm. What did she say that could make this better? The limo went faster on the highway.

Gigi swallowed, and she slumped her shoulders. "Thank you."

He rearranged his seat nearest the door. Gigi scooted further in, and sat next to Erica and the window. She reached up to finger her necklace, but she stopped and dropped her hand then straightened her clothes.

Gigi swung her gaze back to her students. Erica's parents were religious, and Erica never got to travel to see her own country. The girl stared outside with wide-eyed wonder, and Gigi understood her implied promise to keep an extra close watch on her. Erica stared continued on to Raphael, the Puerto Rican boy in her French class. Raphael never noticed Erica, but Gigi could sense the girl's innocent crush.

Erica whispered, "I thought for sure yesterday this wasn't going to happen, Ms. Dumont."

"No. Have faith in people and your dreams." Gigi's gaze took in Sean's intense blue eyes. Once she could have been his.

"You, too. Maybe you'll get married one day, Ms. Dumont."

Gigi crossed her arms. "We don't need relationships to make us whole."

Erica laughed. "Mr. Collins is nice and he watches out for you and he's hot, Ms. Dumont. Marry him," Erica said loudly.

Gigi cringed as Sean laughed.

Gigi flinched. She'd once believed in fairy tales. Stealing a glance at Sean, she spotted lines on his face that made him appear overtired. He used to get cranky without a bagel in the morning. She rubbed her eyes and bit her lip. Why did she remember that?

She sighed, straightened her shoulders, and avoided his gaze for the rest of the ride.

After about twenty minutes, she turned toward the students and said, "After we check in, let's head to the Eiffel Tower. Walking will be nice."

Cheers sounded throughout the limo.

Sean smiled, though the fatigue lines near his eyes gave his true state away. Empathy swelled in her chest when she thought how he'd almost died. Cancer sucked, but he didn't look sick. He had his hair, a great tan, and his sexy, kissable lips. His strong arms had once made everything else in her life disappear. The disease had aged him, but the overall passage of time had made him hotter and rugged. Would he still make her body tremble in desire?

Wait.

She rolled her shoulders. She had no right to daydream about him.

She forced her gaze onto the excited teenagers.

The white streets and fashionable people in the square gave her an idea of where she was. Trocodero Circle. She parted her lips, but her mouth was so dry. She cleared her throat then asked, "Hotel's around here?"

Sean read something on his phone for a second, "No, but we're getting close. We're staying on Avenue de Montaigne on the other side of the Seine, on the way to the Champs-Elysee."

"Near the Arch De Triumphe?"

"Walking distance."

His hotel must be luxurious. The exclusive location sounded dreamy.

Erica asked loudly, "When you lived here, Ms. Dumont, did you leave near there?"

"No. I basically lived in the outskirts of Paris and for a millisecond in Chinatown. This is the rich people section," she replied.

"You lived here?" Sean raised a brow at her.

Hadn't he known? Her heart fell in her chest. But they'd never spoken again. Smiling up at him, she answered, "*Oui, monsieur. Deux ans.*"

He stared straight at her and her courage wavered. The limo hit a small bump and then drove over the short, decorated bridge above the Seine. *Oohs* and *ahs* echoed in the back seat.

The limo slowed to a stop at a white marble mansion that had been transformed into luxury hotel. They piled out and Gigi took in a deep breath of air.

Sean offered his hand. She accepted, then coughed.

So much for elegance.

Sean hadn't noticed. "Let's put our stuff in our rooms and meet downstairs in the lobby in ten minutes. No one is to bring more than twenty-five euro on their person."

Gigi understood. Theft happened every day there. Blinking, she added, "No purses. We can come back here to get money for dinner."

The students paid them no attention and stared in awe at the whitewashed gleaming hotel.

"The hotel used to be an elegant, imperial theater designed for Napoleon," Sean explained. "But we transformed into a posh hotel."

"And we get to stay here?" Kendra's eyes brightened and took a step to go inside. The others followed Kendra.

Erica stayed firmly planted on the sidewalk outside, and her jaw hadn't quite closed. Gigi came over and stood next to Erica, her favorite student. "Are you good?"

"This is beautiful. I don't want to touch anything."

"Go ahead, Erica. For a week, we live here."

The girl didn't budge. "I don't know how."

Gigi took the girl's hand in hers and whispered, "Pretend you're one of the rich girls off on an adventure in Paris from your novels."

"I'll try." Erica nodded then skipped off with her friends into the lobby.

Sean carried a bag over his shoulder and waited for her. Imagining him carrying her in his arms, Gigi felt the heat in her cheeks grow warm. His lips moved. She stared blankly then realized he'd said something. "What?"

He pressed his back into the wall and asked, "With all your money, why would you live in the working-class neighborhood?"

"I cut off communication with Mom for years," she answered without looking at him. "She had money, not me. And she had no idea where I lived or what I did."

"Lillian never said anything." His voice beckoned her to look up. He tugged at his collar, and gave her a glimpse of his strong neck. Her mouth grew dry as he held open the elevator door for her. "What did you want to talk about?"

Talk? Her eyes were on his broad shoulders. Smoothing out her black pants, she remembered. "I wanted to know if we could split the night shift. Tomorrow night, I, umm, I want to go out."

He dropped his bag at the elevator, and he breathed faster now. "You want to go out?"

"Yes."

Gigi kept her gaze on the door. She couldn't explain. She needed to keep her outrageous former roommate, Cary, who might show up as Donna, his alter ego, separate from the students. She met Sean's big blue eyes. "We can trade nights off, right?"

The elevator dinged open and she stepped inside. Sean grabbed his bag and joined her, "We're one floor below the penthouse, but the students can use the penthouse for practice. I had the staff set up a debate stage."

"You're using the most expensive room at this place for students to have a debate room?" The price alone would have paid for her rent in Paris for a year. When he didn't reply, she said, "You have to be losing money. We can practice outside for free."

"Your students get few perks for being part of your winning team, Gigi. Let me make this an extra-special trip for them. It won't cost me a dime since I own the place." He smiled at her. He made life look easy with that grin. "Don't argue over this."

The elevator doors opened on their floor. Losing her focus, she'd give him anything he wanted at the moment. "I want to go to my room and be alone for thirty seconds."

Sean shrugged and followed her down the hall. She pretended not to notice how his footsteps echoed so close to hers. "How did the students know their rooms and I don't?"

Sean stared at her like she was five. "You were helping Erica stay calm, and I checked us in. I take it she doesn't have a lot of money."

Oh. Her mouth dropped open. "You're right, but then most people aren't the Collins family."

He pointed in the hallway. "The boys are in the room across from me. The girls are in the two rooms across from us. You're here." He tapped on a door.

"This is all really nice, Sean, but what did you tell the parents about these changes? We have to follow rules, Sean."

"You know I don't like rules, but don't worry. When I called the parents last night, I went over all the details and also emailed each and every one of them an itinerary." He gave her arm a little shake. "So stop worrying, okay?"

He winked at her.

"Okay," she agreed with a sigh. She turned away from his intense gaze and inserted her plastic card into the electronic key reader. The green light flashed, and she used her knee to hold open the door.

Sean stepped next door and did the same thing. She stared at him until he said, "Fifteen minutes, Scout."

She gulped. There was no escape.

Chapter 6

Gigi waited in the hotel lobby for the rest of the group. The six girls and she had been on time. But the men were late. Wasn't it supposed to be the other way around?

Kendra and Erica remained in a deep conversation, and the other four girls chatted and giggled. Everyone sounded excited. Gigi squared her shoulders every time she saw that the elevator reached the lobby level. How could she spend so much time with Sean and not be affected? She'd have to be on guard every moment.

Today they would get used to the time change, visit the Eiffel Tower.

The ding of the elevator turned her head and she stared at the doors. A second later, Sean stepped off looking like a million dollars in a fresh-pressed shirt. The boys were with him.

Gigi's eyes widened in surprise, and her body heated up at the way Sean's muscles moved beneath that white crisp shirt.

With a grin at the other boys, Sean put his sunglasses on with his right hand then ran his left hand through his hair. The boys did the same move a few seconds later. Gigi giggled and the girls rolled their eyes and huffed.

Ignoring the throbbing in her lower body and planting a wide smile on her face, Gigi turned toward the girls. "Let's get going."

Sean called out, "I requested a car."

"No." If she had to sit next to him again, she'd faint from overheating. "It's a twenty-minute walk, and we wore our sneakers. Let's get going. When we go out of the hotel, head south, then take the first right on Avenue Montaigne."

Sean rushed beside her and waved toward the students. "Stay in front of us. Look for the Eiffel Tower, and we'll keep heading in that direction."

Heads bobbed in agreement. Why had he chimed in? Had she confused anyone? Her eyes darted around as the students followed his directions. So much for being the best chaperone. She turned her nose up at him, but he kept pace with her. "I thought about what you said, Gigi."

"What did I say?" She moved in step with a man hotter than any movie star, a man whose body she'd once known in intimate detail. She felt her body temperature rise and a prickle of sweat rose along her spine, making her hands clammy.

"I have a huge favor to ask," Sean said as they walked. "Can you go out tonight instead? I'll need tomorrow."

"I wanted tomorrow," she argued. Did he have a date? Tilting her head sideways, she pushed the envelope with him to get her way. "I made plans."

"I'm asking a favor. I know it." He paused, as if deciding whether or not to elaborate, then said, "My brother Daniel has a medical convention in Geneva. He's stopping over in Paris for dinner, and I wanted to catch up with him."

"Ohh." He didn't have a date. Her shoulders dropped, but her heart raced. If he kept whispering in her ear, she'd implode. He was too sexy. "When's the last time you saw Daniel? Last week at the family compound?"

"He's a doctor, just out of the Marines. He'll be setting up practice at home soon enough, but I haven't seen him since I was laid up in my hospital bed."

"Why?" Her voice fluttered. All the Collins men had spent time in the marines, though she had no idea what drove them there.

"He's been stationed abroad. Liam's always on some mission, and Gerard is usually super busy. Seeing each other takes effort."

The love in Sean's eyes made her chest tighten. She didn't have that. Never had. Stepping back to give him space, she stared straight ahead then nodded. "Fine. I'll change my plans."

Sean's eyebrow rose. "So how exactly did you plan on seeing your friend when you were the only chaperone till yesterday?"

She ground her teeth then told him the truth. "I told him to be on standby just in case. He has a flexible schedule, so you go see your brother."

His hand grazed her arm, and she inhaled a deep woodsy smell of his soap. He nodded. "Thank you. I'm sure your friend will be happy to see you."

Sean had no idea. Cary preferred men, but she smiled back. "Great, I'll have my date tonight then."

"I thought he was a friend." Sean stopped in his tracks.

Her pulse cooled and she leaned away. "Yes, friends with my favorite man in all of Paris."

Sean's forehead grew, and she shrugged her shoulders. Good.

She remained silent and took another cool step.

They rounded the corner onto the short bridge, and the students raced ahead.

A smile broke out on her face. She'd love to expel her energy, and she called behind her shoulder, "I'm going to run ahead," she said. "We need to stay with them."

He winked at her. "I'll beat you."

"You want to race?" She hesitated for a second, and her heart beat faster.

Sean's boyish smile took her breath away. "We both know I'll win."

She sprinted forward, with her feet pounding on the pavement. She shrieked back, "We do? You're on."

She screamed out her joy every moment she stayed ahead. The children all stayed together, and Gigi intended to rush through them. She enjoyed the playful competition, and her head spun.

Then she stepped off the street corner. Her heart slammed into her throat as a car appeared out of nowhere, barreling straight toward her. She started to back away then Sean's arms circled her waist, forcing her back abruptly back onto the sidewalk. Trembling with the surge of adrenaline, she stared at him wide-eyed.

He'd saved her. Sean had saved her!

"Ms. Dumont," one of the students called. "Are you okay?"

"Y-y-yes," she called. "Tell everyone to stay there. We'll be along in a minute."

"Are you okay, Gigi? Bastard was speeding."

The low timbre of Sean's voice sent a shiver down her spine.

She gulped. No, she wasn't okay. She ached to fling her arms around Sean. He had saved her, but then he'd always been her hero.

Too bad she'd screwed over their relationship, their future and potential happiness.

Chapter 7

Sean rubbed his neck and tried to clamp down the lust thrumming through his body. It wasn't the first time he had stared at Gigi's curves from behind. In high school, she'd been the prettiest girl in school, but she'd been thin. Now the woman in front of him standing in line to buy tickets for the students had curves that had become more defined; her butt rounder, and her legs more interesting. If she gained even another ten or twenty pounds, those features would enhance.

"Sean, are you listening to a word I say?"

Hell, he hadn't even noticed she'd moved to stand next to him, tickets in hand.

He blinked. "Sorry, Scout, what did you say?"

Her arms tightened around her waist again and she automatically reached for her necklace. His gaze focused on the gold band and recognition dawned in his eyes. "Is that—?" *my high school ring?*

"Don't be ridiculous." She interrupted fast, and hid the necklace under her shirt. "And let's use formalities from now, Mr. Collins."

His eyebrow shot up. "What did you say?"

"You don't listen to anything."

He smirked. Yes, he did. He'd chose a battle with her later. Stripping her to her underwear and seeing his ring on her neck sounded fun, but he couldn't. Instead, he kept his hand on his hip. "What?"

"The children are in line for the elevator, and you're holding us up."

He turned on his heels and followed her. He kept his

eyes on her shoulders and only periodically lowered his gaze to her hot gluteus maximus. The second the elevator doors closed, the teenagers stepped back and their mouths dropped again at the sights of the city.

Sean smiled as they ascended higher.

Kendra took a step back, and Sean chuckled at their shock. "Not many open-air elevators in Hyannis Port."

Gigi's stillness indicated her claustrophobia. Poor thing still suffered after all these years.

He dropped his hands when the elevator stopped and the crowd thinned out presenting them with an amazing view of the city of Paris through the floor-to-ceiling windows.

If he squinted, Sean thought he could see the Champs De Elysee and noticed how the buildings glistened white and pure in the bright sun.

He took out his phone to snap a picture for his son. One day his son, Patrick, would want to be here.

After he got the shot he wanted, he glanced to his side, and his skin turned ashen. Gigi wiped a tear out of her eye. Why would she cry? He put his phone away in his pocket and went to her side. "Are you okay?"

"Shh. It's nothing to concern yourself with." Her voice choked. "Nothing at all."

"It's not nothing." Ignoring her made his life easier, but she needed help. For one minute, he'd drop his guard. If she let him, he'd hold her. Standing next to her, he asked, "What's making you cry?"

"Regrets." She stared up at him, and squeezed her eyes shut.

He tugged her arm. "Follow me. We'll have some privacy in this corner. You don't want the children to see you."

Her shoulders drooped. "Okay."

He found them a quiet corner then rubbed her shoulder and back. "You aren't thinking about the past now?"

She rubbed her eyes. "I always do here. This was the last place I ever had time with just my dad. Lilian . . ."

"I never understood how you were related to her, and don't pretend affection now. Not after how she treated you."

She nodded. "You're right."

"Don't give the woman another thought." He paused then said, "You must have gone to college, Gigi."

She nodded and stared out into the city. "I did. I lived here for two years then moved to Miami. Mom agreed to pay for college if I moved back to the United States, like that would make me visit her. I never did. Every summer and winter break, I came back here, avoiding her. Then . . ."

His ears sharpened for clues on the mystery. Gigi had cut him so cold at his party. She sighed then continued, "I moved here again for six months then Venice for a year before hopping back to Paris and New York."

"Lilian at least paid for school."

Gigi balled her hand into a fist. "Mom cut me off when I moved to Paris, and I stuck it out here in defiance. I let her bail me out when I lived in New York and Miami. I used to hate asking her for a dime, but sometimes I had no other choice." She unballed her fists then groaned. "Well that's my story. You did your service, then stayed home, married, had your son, and somehow added teacher to the resume. The teaching gig makes no sense for you."

He crossed his arms. "I was used for my money, and wanted to live without it." For some reason, Gigi forced honesty out of him. He'd never even told his own mother. Sean ran his hands through his hair and met her curious gaze. "My wife didn't like me much." He paused. "Unlike you, I stayed home, in Cape Cod. We vacationed, wherever Jennifer wanted, until the year I became a teacher. Home remained my center. She didn't want that."

One of the teenagers waved at them both. Sean waved back.

"I was wrong not to trust you."

The arrow shot right at his defenses.

"We were the biggest mistake in my life," she said softly. "I should never have walked away."

"What?" The question fell out of his mouth and his vision darkened.

Sean shrugged and kept his voice cold. "Can't do anything about the past." Gigi should have come to him a long time ago, but she hadn't cared. "You didn't—"

She touched his hand and sparks hit him hard. "I could have been stronger."

Sean shook his head and finally stepped away. "I'd have taken care of us, and stood up to Lillian. You must have known that."

"No, Sean, I—" Tears filling her eyes, Gigi hastened away to another quiet section of the Eiffel Tower while he struggled to gather his wits.

A uniformed guard approached him. "Are you with the American student group?" "Yes." Sean snapped back to the present. "What happened?"

"I told the woman near the elevator that the students went down a few minutes ago."

"Thanks."

Sean rushed to the elevator then joined Gigi inside as the doors closed. His gaze darted around. They were alone. Gigi stepped back to the wall "I thought you took them downstairs without me."

Sean shook his head. "No, I wouldn't do that."

The elevator jerked to a stop. Gigi swerved, and almost toppled forward. He grabbed the banister near her and held her back. "Are you okay?"

"I'm good. Just the worst chaperone in the world. What happened?"

Her warm breath caught him in surprise, and the smell of her flowery perfume caught in his lungs.

"The elevator stopped."

"Why?"

Her face paled and she glanced at her phone. No service. But she texted something, but she wasn't sure she called her provider to ensure her phone worked. She closed her eyes, hoped, then turned around. He stepped away and stared down the steep outdoor decline of the tower. He trusted technology, but Gigi was claustrophobic. His face twisted back to her fast, to ensure she held together. But as he gazed at her, his heart thumped in his chest. He needed to move past Gigi. Being stuck with her wouldn't go well.

"Don't look down," she told herself.

Her eyes stared out the window. Her eyes went wide.

"Geegs, Look at me."

"You're safe."

Her shoulders hunched together and she took a deep breath. Finally the color returned to her cheeks. "I should have given you a chance to say something I'm sorry. My habit is to run."

"You're sorry?" Am I supposed to be okay with 'sorry'?" Her perfume swirled around in his lungs, and rose in his throat. He choked on the air and breathed fire to stop the smell. "No. You don't get to apologize for what you did with just 'I'm sorry.'"

"What else am I supposed to say?" She gnawed her lower lip. "I should have been able to say no? I wish I had."

He took a step toward her and she held firm. He inhaled her sweet berry soap. And his mouth watered. He'd intended to speak his mind, but instead, his fingers stroked her back. Then a fire consumed him, and he lowered his mouth hers.

Her hand played with his hair, then drew him closer. She tasted better than homemade cookies sprinkled on a sundae. Her dewy lips stole away his anger. But he couldn't let himself go. He'd not forget or forgive her. Instead, he tore himself out of her arms, and wiped his lips. She panted and he clenched his jaw. He had no right. She had left him.

"Why did you kiss me?" Her words came out breathy and unsure.

At first he had no answer. He wanted to lash out or kiss her again. Then he replied, "It was either that or kill you, Gigi. I'm not sure I made the right choice."

Chapter 8

Gigi could almost feel the steam coming out of her ears. Had Sean really say such a thing? Sean? Yes, she'd screwed up their lives, ten years ago, but kiss her or kill her?

Her palms tingled. *He'd chosen kiss.* She stepped into his space and traced her body as she had trailed her hand up to his strong body to his neck. She pouted and invited him to kiss her. With a sigh, she parted her lips and she took in his hot breath on her body, and shivered.

He resisted her until she stood on her toes and brought his mouth crashing into hers.

A damn must have burst inside of him because he kissed her back. Good. She gasped. Then he shoved her against the cold metallic wall and her body heat steamed her. Every nerve cell in her body craved his touch. She matched his rising passion, kiss for kiss. And she needed more. She slipped her hand under his shirt to graze her fingers on his smooth back. His bare skin sent her into a liquid state.

His mouth lowered to kiss the upper curve of her breast then sucked on her neck. His fingers played with her necklace, but she didn't care. Her breasts ached. He could do anything he wanted to her provided he never stopped.

Her head dropped back, giving him full access to her neck. His moans mirrored her own. Funny. Her body trusted Sean. A sigh escaped her mouth in mimic. Then he drew away from her neck and his lips returned to hers.

His hands raked her back, and tugged her clean shirt out of her black pants. But all she imagined was wrapping her legs around his waist.

The elevator rocked, but she held onto his neck to keep him with her. Grinding her hips forward, and encountered his fullness. She tugged out his shirt, and her fingers itched to remove the unnecessary boundary between them.

Having him inside her would answer years of prayers. It wasn't until the chime next to her ear rang, and sunlight filled her eyes that she realized they . . . The students! The thought worked like a cold bucket of water to calm her hormones. With trembling hands, she slipped her shirt on, and ran her hand through her tangled mess of her hair. Sean tucked his shirt back in, stared hard at her, and then blocked her from any potential eyes until she finished dressing.

Still the gentleman.

Even now, she ached for him to continue. Her body was like a furnace and she needed something cold. She glanced around the open green field. No water spigot in sight. She licked her lips. She needed something cold to stop the fire in her body.

She knew her skin must be flushed, too. Sighing, she took hold of her mind. Kissing Sean made no sense. He should hate her. Kissing Sean would end in heartbreak.

Propelling her forward, Sean pushed away from the door, and she immediately spotted her students. She frowned. "Something's wrong with this picture." Why would they all be sitting on a park bench and smile at them innocently and sweetly?

He followed her stare then whispered, "How long were we in the elevator?"

She glanced at her phone and her heart sank. "Twenty minutes."

"It felt like two."

Her heart thumped hard against her chest. How had she lost track of time? And all Sean had done was kiss her.

"Could your students have locked us in there?"

Her neck snapped toward him. *Of course not* was on the tip of her tongue then she stopped and stared back at the angelic teenagers. "Why would you think they'd trick us?"

"Kendra, David, and Erica watched me holding your hand on our way up. I brushed off the conspiracy theory, but their faces so damn innocent. See, look at how their hands are folded in their laps. Patrick acts sweet when he's manipulating me for more cookies, and he's only three."

But the students had no idea about their history.

Sean led her closer to the teenagers and their pasted smiles of *'we're sweet and innocent.'* Gigi raised her eyebrow and narrowed in on Erica, sitting with her hand under Raphael's. Erica would crack under pressure.

"Let's get going," Sean said, gesturing for the teens to rise. "You must be hungry."

"I'm not hungry," Kendra answered. "But it *would* be good to practice for the competition before dinner and then sightsee after. We want to win."

"Let's sightsee a bit then go back to the hotel," Gigi suggested. Glancing at Sean, she felt her cheeks flush. "Mr. Collins set up a room for us."

His eyes laughed at her.

After spending time exploring the area surrounding the Eiffel Tower, they marched back the same way they came. Erica stayed close to Gigi and Sean kept himself in the back. When no one was nearby, Erica whispered to her, "Ms. Dumont, your shirt is unbuttoned."

Gigi stopped and stared down. Her shirt was open at her waist. And been for about an hour. With a giggle, Erica rushed forward to join the students while Gigi turned to her side and, moving fast, tucked in her shirt.

Sean Collins was far too dangerous for her sanity. In a few days, this would all end and they go back to their separate lives.

Chapter 9

The French competition wasn't just a foreign spelling be. The team had to be fluent and able to answer obscure facts about France. Gigi's heart and body lost their knots. Practice went well and her students had spoken beautifully this evening. Positivity filled her lungs, and her students made her laugh until enough stomachs growled. "Practice is over. Go to your room and meet in the lobby in fifteen minutes."

Gigi lagged behind and picked up the suite after them. Candy wrappers and soda cans followed teenagers wherever they appeared. When she finished cleaning, she took the elevator downstairs to her room to quickly change.

In the halls, she heard laughter from the girls' room and then from the boys' room. She knocked on the girls' door. Someone opened it and she peeked inside. The girls spun around in cute spring dresses. She shook her head and left. Then she did the same with the boys' room. She knocked, and Raphael called out, "Don't come in. We're getting dressed."

Gigi swallowed then decided to find out about Sean and his brother. She hesitated at his door with her hand in the air. She took a deep breath, then knocked. No answer. She knocked again. Had Sean left without a goodbye?

She turned to go to her room when she heard a clink of bolts. She stepped back, and had been prepared for many possibilities, but not for this. Her jaw dropped. Sean Collins' naked, chiseled rock-hard chest hadn't been on her list. Better than any statue of a god. Her body steamed up fast. She stepped backward then cleared her throat. "We're hungry for dinner now. You want to go with us?"

"Let me grab my shirt." He stepped into his room, but left the door open, and called out, explaining, "My son, Patrick, kept talking to me. I think he's afraid I abandoned him."

What could she say right now? *Put a shirt on? Keep it off and let me rub every muscle?* Neither sounded much like what she should say, though the latter sent shivers of desire down her body.

Gigi flinched.

"I miss my parents," Erica piped in from behind, and Gigi's mouth almost dropped. "How old is your son?"

"Patrick is three."

"Your wife must be great," Erica replied.

Words escaped Gigi's capabilities at the moment. She breathed in and out, then explained, "Mr. Collins's wife died about a year ago. His grandparents are watching his son, allowing Mr. Collins to be our male chaperone."

"Glad I get to meet a few students at my new school." Sean stepped out of his room and finished with his buttons of his shirt. "How did practice go?"

Gigi blinked for one second. What had he asked? Her mind stayed fuzzy then she slowly focused. "Awesome. Tonight the students will order everything we eat, and the tour will be in French."

"You're ordering for me then."

Gigi nodded, and her eyes stayed on his fingers.

The second he buttoned his last button, he winked at her.

Her gaze lowered. Thankfully Erika had returned to her room for the others. Gigi's felt her face grow warm. Sean's pants seemed to stretch a bit tighter in the front and his lower extremities became more defined. For the last ten years, she'd compared every man she ever knew to him. How could she stop looking now?

"Ms. Dumont, I'm hungry." Kendra's whiney princess voice called from the direction of the elevator, effectively destroying her sex fantasy.

"Give me a sec to change," Gigi called then hastened to her room. Thankfully she'd set everything out beforehand. A quick change and a dash of makeup later she was ready for a night on the town. A few minutes later, she joined them as they getting into the limo again.

"Tomorrow we have to navigate the subway. They need to develop map skills to take care of themselves in the future."

"You figured out the subway when we didn't grow up near one," Sean commented in a quiet voice.

"I had no choice." She crowded in the corner and kept her hands on her chin. Cary had saved her the day she arrived there. "An angel guided me and adopted me."

"You found religion, too?" His eyes widened.

She laughed. "No. A human angel." She doubted Sean would understand. He'd never struggled for anything. Well, he'd had his medical issues, but money had never motivated him or scared him. She pasted on a smile and faced the students until the limo stopped. "We must be here."

"David, when you go inside, give them my name," Sean told the boy. "My French is bad."

The students filed out and into the fancy restaurant.

At the door of the restaurant, Erica tugged Gigi's arm.

"I can't afford to eat here. I'll go get a burger and meet you back here in an hour."

Gigi shook her head. "We're not separating. I'll cover you."

"Ms. Dumont, you're the best teacher I ever had. But this place smells expensive. Look. I'll pay you back"

"Nonsense." Gigi glanced over her shoulder, and she saw how Sean had kept the boys surrounding him while they waited for them. Gigi smiled then told Erica, "It's my treat, really. Let's go join the others."

Within second of stepping inside the glass doors, Erica bounded off. Raphael saved the seat next to him for Erica, and Gigi nodded for her to go ahead.

Sean came up behind Gigi and asked, "Is everything okay?"

"She's worried about the cost. Look around. This place isn't where teenagers go." she told him, though she didn't expect him to understand.

He put his hand on hers for a second and whispered, "I'm buying dinner for everyone."

"You don't have to pay for everything. We have a budget."

Sean smiled, and she stared at his beautiful white teeth. "I changed the plans and I'll pay the price."

"Thank you," she said then settled into her seat.

The students looked at the menu, thankfully unaware of anything going on between her and Sean.

Sean dropped his napkin on his lap and stared at the menu.

A few minutes later, Kendra asked, "Ms. Dumont, do you think this place has a *prix fixe* menu? What if we don't have enough to cover the cost?"

Sean smiled. "I'm buying. It's my gift for letting me join you at the last minute."

"But Ms. Dumont roped you into going," Raphael said. "You don't have to pay for everything."

"Ms. Dumont?" Sean raised a brow. "She didn't make me buy the school."

"Raphael, Kendra, stop." Erica's face went red as she confessed, "You're being nice. And we're sorry. We thought you must like each other. We were encouraging you."

Sean glanced in her direction and raised his eyebrow. "I'll need everyone's word. We're here for a nice dinner, but neither Ms. Dumont nor I will be the subject of schemes."

"Are you sure?" Raphael said with a smirk. "You both looked like you had a good time."

Gigi covered her face with her palm. The boy hadn't learned to keep his smart comments to himself. Normally she'd laugh, but Sean deserved better.

"Ms. Dumont had more than earned your respect, and you should show her that," Sean said. "Now let's have dinner."

Breathe in, then out. Repeat. The butterflies in her stomach sped up. Slowly, Gigi sank back in her chair. Her eyes narrowed and she realized she could be calm. He hadn't been upset.

The students nodded in agreement and Sean smiled at everyone then sat down. He played with his hair, sipped his water, and stared at his menu. The students followed his lead.

Gigi's fingers itched to caress his knees under the table but the daydreams had to stop. A moment later, she added, "Let's order dinner. David, order the duck for me."

Sean closed his menu, and stroked his throat. "The lamb dinner for me. Raphael, please order me that. The picture on the menu looks good."

The teenagers made cross-eyed faces to each other and gave that vibe that adults were weird. Gigi laughed, sipped her water, and finally her stomach stopped flipping.

Then Sean patted her knee.

Gigi's lips formed a circle, but she couldn't say a word. The boys ordered for the teachers and the rest of the group ordered for themselves.

Raphael face went white as the waitress told him, "*Non.*"

He bit his lips and tried to order his cheeseburger and macaroni again.

The waitress again said, "*Non.*"

Gigi fought a grin as Raphael let it go and ordered something on the menu. The waitress left and the group perked up.

Sean leaned closer to her, and whispered in her ear, "I should have noticed your shirt before we left the elevator. It won't happen again."

"What won't?" she asked with a breathy voice.

His eyebrow quirked up. "Both, I'd imagine, Geegs. It's what you want?"

No. Yes. A flush of heat rose to her cheeks and she stole a glance at Sean. Then she licked her lips at the memory of the kiss flashed. She froze then quickly sipped her water, though it did nothing to stem her desire for the man sitting way too nearby. "I'm starved."

Sean signaled for a waiter and told Raphael to order bread. Raphael grinned and placed the request.

Gigi swiveled in her chair. "How did you know?"

"I have a son. I could tell Raphael needed to be empowered a little."

Gigi stroked her arm, and wished she had the guts to touch him.

Soon the waiter brought over bread, and Sean directed with his hands that the first piece should be Gigi's. After chewing on her first bite, Gigi's curiosity took over. "What happened with Jennifer? Can you talk about it?"

"Jennifer wanted my money, and in exchange she gave me Patrick. She threatened to leave years before she did. Finally she walked out the house, went to the bank, took out a large sum of cash, and bought herself a plane ticket."

"Where were you?" Gigi asked.

"I was at work, teaching economics at the high school."

Gigi brushed her hand on his arm, but didn't dare hold him. "Wow. So what happened? I thought she died."

"She did." Sean stopped and took a sip of his water. He swallowed then continued. "The police informed me six months ago they found her body in Los Angeles. She'd been mugged." He frowned. "I always assumed she was on her way to Tibet. She said she needed to go there to study with the monks, but I don't really care."

"You have the family you wanted. A son." Gigi

offered him a small smile. "And she named her after your grandfather."

Sean gave a short, mocking laugh then ate another piece of bread. His face dark and brooding, he chewed in silence.

The children were unaware of the tension, and Gigi kept her hands in her lap. Finally Sean said, "Jennifer signed off on her parental rights in her good-bye letter for me, where she stated she stayed in town to take my money and run, which proved to me how stupid I had been."

"She didn't?" Dumbfounded, Gigi stared at him. Her hand curled into a fist as she pictured herself defending Sean. "I'm sorry."

His eyes hollowed, and his face masked any emotion. He shook his head then shrugged. "You should understand her reasoning," he murmured.

Before she could reply, the waitress arrived with the food.

Gigi didn't move a muscle. She tried to eat, but the food didn't sit right in her stomach. Caring about Sean would end in disaster for him and her. And they'd already been down that road.

Chapter 10

Sean stared at Gigi, who wasn't eating. He hadn't meant to hurt her with his comment. Or maybe he had. He blew out a breath. Part of him still hoped to get far away from her and their past. But she had to eat. He nudged Gigi's plate of untouched food toward her. She glared at him, unmoving. But she was too skinny. He leaned closer to Gigi. "The waiters do not bring the bill to the table, Gigi, until everyone is done with the food. They will think you hated it or that you're a rude American."

"I know that." Gigi stared up at him. "How do you?"

"I came here on vacation once or twice." He stared pointedly at her cutlery.

"There isn't much on anyone's plate, Ms. Dumont," Kendra said encouragingly. "Even if you aren't hungry, it's delicious."

With a nod, Gigi picked up her fork at their urgings and slowly chewed her food. Sean watched as she grinned and color slowly reappeared in her cheeks. Good. About fifteen minutes later, the students seemed eager to leave, but he kept them in their seats. "After dinner we have a night tour and a stop at Napoleon's tomb."

"Are there ghosts?" David asked, his eyes wide open.

The girls in the seats next to him both jumped.

"Don't scare the women. You know better, son." Sean smiled at the boy.

After she finished eating Gigi ushered the hyper teenagers to the restroom and he dealt with the check. A few of the boys waited with him and he let them talk to waiter. They explained in French that Cape Cod was not near California, and not Virginia. The waiter asked how far from Los Angeles there home was, and they answered Boston was nowhere close. His heart grew swelled. The level of comprehension the students had impressed him. Gigi had worked hard and it showed. After they returned, he'd see she was rewarded. And a smile grew on his face.

Once outside, Sean led the group to a waiting tour bus on the side street near the restaurant. The students bounded on but Kendra sounded disappointed. "What happened to the limo?"

Gigi placed her hand on Sean's forearm and his skin grew goosebumps. "This has windows for everyone to see out of, and a guide to explain the city."

The girl's face fell down to her shoulders.

Sean lifted his chin and was tempted to call the town car for a personalized tour. Gigi made a noise, and ushered everyone on board. He stared and his eyes must have grown wider. Her backside made his hand itch to grab her. And her tight black skirt showed off her curves.

Last on board, he took the seat in the front. The students spaced out. The young female tour guide winked at him, and he saw Gigi freeze in place. He would have brushed it off but the tour guide said, "Your wife is unhappy, sir. I didn't know about her."

Sean must have gazed too long at the young woman because Gigi came toward him with her arms crossed. "Is there an issue?"

"Scout, sit down next to me." He took her hand in his and helped her sit. Before she could complain, he whispered in her ear, "The guide believes we're married."

"You should have corrected her," she scolded with pinched lips, then stood up to find another seat.

"Gigi, I'm not looking to complicate my life. Please stay," he asked as she blinked at him. "I need you."

He kept his gaze glued to her. She stared past him and toward the guide. Then she dropped her arms and settled into her seat beside him. The bus driver turned on the engine, and she whispered to him, "I don't know if she'll buy our act."

"Don't be stupid. I'd have married you at age five given the option." The truth rang in his own ears. Married her before she'd murdered all his hopes and dreams.

Gigi sat there stiff and uncomfortable for a long time. The guide pointed out the Place du Chatelet describing that most of the prisons near the Grand Chatelet were destroyed during the revolution.

Two hours later, the bus turned toward Napoleon's Camp near the Eiffel Tower. They'd be back to the hotel in less than ten minutes. Sean's muscles tightened. Gigi would leave for her date then. He stood up and addressed the group. "Let's get out for a few minutes."

"What?" Gigi asked.

He squelched his desire to mouth off that her favorite French man had nothing. Instead, he surprised everyone and ushered the teenagers off the bus. Gigi glared at him but he'd use this as a delay tactic till he thought of something better. Yes. He knew this wasn't mature, and he didn't care. With a smile, he said, "After we take pictures, we can go to a café for pastry before bed."

Cheers from the teenagers turned Gigi's frown into a grin. So much for French everything. Sean kept his gloat to himself and told himself to stop. Sure, he deserved someone who loved him and a family. And Gigi would never fit that bill. But his sex drive hoped to continue where they'd left off in the elevator. Gigi Dumont used to be his everything, and now he wanted his life back.

Chapter 11

Gigi's head fell to her side. Sean kept stalling her. Why? He couldn't want to spend time with her, and he couldn't be jealous. Gigi straightened her clothes and stalled. She had no answer, but she knew in her heart that he cared a little. She shook her head. No way would he. Then she straightened up.

"You can see how Napoleon trained his troops to be an efficient fighting force, can't you?" Sean, his back to her, asked one of the students. "Battle formations began over there."

The boys pretended to understand the ways of wars and soon the girls began to yawn. Kendra, the leader of the pack, asked, "Can we go to the café now? I want to drink a real *cafe au lait* and people watch."

Gigi suppressed her smile. Kendra would be bored in three to five minutes of *'people watching.'* She lived her life out loud and in color. Somehow Kendra would transform a simple sit-down to some action-packed event.

Gigi smiled and called over to Sean, "Let's get going to the café."

A few minutes later, the boys rejoined them on the bus. Sean brushed his hand on Gigi's, adjusted his body next to her, then took his seat again. Her body warmed from his simple nearness. Awareness of him made her ache. She plopped into her seat beside him, but held her body stiff. "You bring a different energy to this trip. I'm glad you're here."

"Scout, I came here to help you. Now let's get that coffee." He patted her cold hand. "Relax."

Her mouth opened to argue with him about the nickname, but the words wouldn't form. She'd let the familiar nickname slide, though she needed to stop obsessing over him. The cute young tour guide's shadow came over Gigi's seat. She turned to stare up at the girl who winked boldly at Sean. He squeezed Gigi's hand and said, "Thank you for the tour."

"It was my pleasure, Mr. Collins." The girl's French accent gave off a flirting vibe. "You are not married. If you would like a private tour of my home later, I'd be happy to oblige."

"*I* will give Sean a tour of Paris, and it won't include your *'home,'*" Gigi added fast and shoved her hair out of her eyes. The woman glared at her, and Gigi crossed her arms.

Sean raised his eyebrow at her. "I'll take you up on that."

Wait. What happened? Gigi frowned as the girl smiled and walked away. Had she been set up?

The bus stopped and the teenagers piled off to go to the café near the hotel. Gigi tried to stand, but Sean caught and squeezed her hand. The tour guide stepped off the bus then Sean put his hand on her shoulder and whispered, "You were jealous, Gigi. I needed that."

"Don't be stupid. Why should I be jealous?" She huffed out of her seat toward the door, but knew her face must be red. She kept a fast pace and followed the teenagers who filed into the café. Sean joined her a minute later, and took the seat beside her, again. The teenagers all rearranged seats to sit in a group.

Gigi sighed and asked, "You going to laugh at me some more?"

"I wasn't laughing at you. Gigi, we will talk later. Alone."

His seductive blue eyes sent heat inside her that made her knees melt. Damn.

Then he raised the stakes. "Unless you want to talk now."

"No. Later." She couldn't stand being his enemy anymore. She needed to breathe. She closed her eyes, and began to practice her breathing exercises. When she finished, she opened her eyes and whispered, "I'm going to the bathroom."

She scurried away and the students carried on. The second the ladies' room door closed, she stared at herself in the mirror. Her face was hollowed again. Her skin had no luster. No way would Sean ever want her again.

He'd disappear soon enough. She'd wash her hands of their hometown and move to Salt Lake City. No one would know her there, and it would be a fresh start. Disappearing would be good.

Erica entered the ladies' room, and Gigi quickly fluffed her hair. "Ms. Dumont, are you okay? You're glowing, but your eyes say something else."

She glanced in the mirror and stared at her reflection. "I'm fine."

"Good," Erica told her. "You're here in Paris."

Gigi noticed that her cheeks had color today. For some strange reason, that struck a chord. Pasting a smile on her face, Gigi said, "You're right. How could anyone be sad in the greatest city on earth? I'll meet you back outside."

Erica held the door, but the second she stepped foot out of the bathroom door, Gigi met Sean's stare. His blue eyes warmed her. Why? After all she'd done, he shouldn't give her a chance to be near him. He should leave her alone, fire her, and tell her off.

She swallowed. What could she say? *'Kiss me again? Don't mention the past?'* Without any grace, she slid into her seat, but she kept her mouth closed. Then she sniffed and inhaled the rich aroma of the coffee. Only Parisians knew how to make great coffee.

She took a delicious sip. Then she took stock of the students, and noticed a few of them yawning. Today had been a long day, and they hadn't slept since the plane ride. She suppressed a yawn. "Sean, we should get back to the hotel."

Sean sipped his coffee and said, "Have fun on your date tonight."

"Not tonight. Not anymore. I'm too tired."

The intent way he stared at her sent a shiver of desire that rushed through her veins. The tingles grew. *Deep breath. Ignore what he said.* "I'll go the day after tomorrow to see my friend," she added. "That's all. We'll stay another ten minutes, then we'll get them upstairs to their rooms." He nodded and motioned for the waiter and the bill. The students whispered in French and opened up their wallets. Suddenly Sean handed the waiter his card.

The students shrugged and packed their bags. Gigi blinked. Had he paid for everyone again? With her hand on her hip, she said, "The students were required to bring money for incidentals like the café. It's not fair you're paying for everyone."

"I've made a lot more money today than I spent. Don't worry about it." He didn't look at her and signed his name to the receipt.

Her eyes narrowed. "You made money today? How? We've been flying and running around since we landed."

He shrugged. "All I have to do is click a few buttons on my phone. Work isn't hard."

"For you. You majored in business?"

"Accounting and finance, double major. I have my MBA, a masters in economics, and a masters in teaching too. My brain doesn't shut off when it comes to numbers. Until my diagnosis, I stayed out of the family business though I've been well trained."

"At the beginning, I didn't care about college. I was so mad at my mother. But I always enjoyed school, and the longer I stayed, the better I became." She stared at Sean. "You then went to work as Conall Collin's right-hand man?"

He brushed past her body, and the friction sent butterflies in her stomach then nodded. "After being sick, I had nothing else to do and tracked our family and business funds. Making money is easy for me."

"I don't have your financial finesse." She had worked and lived her adult life without money. Now that her mother was dead, she should get that inheritance. One year in a steady job and in her mother's house. She'd do this. She'd prove to her mother's lawyers she deserved the money, then leave. She straightened. "Figuring out how to get the money to do something, and what you are willing to do to achieve it can be a reason to keep on living."

"Ensuring my children are happy and provided for has been my motivation once I passed my rebellious stage of wanting to live like *'normal'* people." He added, "You used to be happier."

"That was a long time ago." Rolling her eyes, she finished her coffee in one sip. "Your mother had money, and still you ran," he whispered. "You don't need to anymore."

"Had. She had money. Most of it she spent to keep up her lifestyle, and I'm fighting to get the rest." Sighing, Gigi refused to meet his eyes. "I don't want to talk about her anymore, Sean."

"Don't go on a date."

Her eyes narrowed on him. "It's not a date. Cary's my roommate, and I owe him my life."

Sean shrugged and sipped the last of his drink. Then he stood up, and offered his hand to help her stand. She accepted and squeezed his fingers for that electrifying moment. Then she stared at the children. "Let's get back to the hotel. In one hour, lights out. Tomorrow you have a practice round on the stage, and we're fitting in more sightseeing."

The quick jaunt to the hotel held no more surprises, and Gigi stopped at the front desk to phone Cary. Sean's eyebrows rose, but he moved to keep his distance. She sighed then left a message, her thoughts scrambled. How could she convince Sean that Cary had always been a friend. And why did that matter so much to her?

Chapter 12

Gigi's heart beat so fast she couldn't think, so she took off right away. Tonight she had plans. She glanced around the small subway. Her night off meant she'd see Cary tonight. Her nose twitched and she traced her arms with her hands. The Paris train system at night had a strange smell of sex in the air. Gigi's face winced every time she had stepped foot on the line and she took in this smell. She sighed. The first time she'd had sex, she'd been young and in love. Sean's lovemaking had been tender, sometimes intense, but always filled with emotion. Now Gigi wrapped her arms around her and her feet rocked on the ground. The sweetest of memories haunted her.

She unwound herself the moment the train stopped at her old stomping ground. Tonight, she'd not think or be near Sean Collins. She de-boarded and followed the exit signs.

How would she survive the week? The man she'd loved as a teen slept one hotel room away from her, and would for the next six days.

She clutched her purse closer to her, and went forward. Tonight she couldn't scratch on Sean's door, even if she wanted to. He'd be sleeping at the time she came home.

Crash.

Glass broke above her head from the apartment building to the right and she heard Cary's infectious laughter. She grinned and her steps grew wider. He must be having one of his infamous parties. Good. A party for an hour or two with old friends would clear her head of Sean Collins.

Music pierced the air of the medieval building on the outskirts of town. At various times in its long history it had been an abbey, a brothel, a hotel, a theater, and a stable. The neighborhood's main draw remained that it was in the middle of nowhere, and the train's last stop. The neighbors would be at the party, and no one ever complained with free-flowing champagne in their hands.

Gigi stepped inside the smoke-filled room. Pushing past guests, Gigi smelled the alcohol. Strange to think she'd drowned out years of sadness from those very glasses.

A booming voice sang out, *"The sweetest woman I ever loved never tasted as good as champagne."*

In his white button-down shirt, folded sleeves, gray tie, and sweater vest, Cary had slightly more gray in his hair now, but he still looked the eternal good boy.

"Idiot." She bowed to Cary and sang back his stupid song, *"So I chose cheap dates and expensive champagne . . ."*

"Gigi!" Cary cried, then waltzed her in a circle to welcome her back then led her to the nearest bar.

She shook her head the second he offered a glass of wine.

His eyebrows shot up. "What, or should I say, *who* has put this glow back in you? You never said no to champagne."

"What? I'm pale and thin." She unbuttoned her matronly sweater and hung it on the counter. "I am not glowing. Don't be crazy."

"Still, there is fire back inside you. Hmm. I know that look. It's a man who has you all worked up." Cary sat her next to him, and insisted she took the glass. She held it, but didn't sip. Then Cary pressed for details. "Is he hot? Rich? Old? No. Not old. You're glowing."

Sean's smile flashed in her eyes and she felt her cheeks flush. "Don't be stupid." She shook her head and repeated, "I am not."

"And in denial, girl." Cary pinched her butt. "Spill. He must be hot. You know I'll get it out of you or go to your hotel."

"Don't you dare." Gigi pushed off the feather boa that fell on them from somewhere. "There is nothing to tell."

"Who is this guy that has you hot and bothered? Will I not approve? Is he gay and impossible for you to get, like me?"

She threw her head back, laughing. "No, Cary. I'm here with my students and, uh, Sean Collins is the other chaperone."

Cary's face grew serious. "Sean Collins? The love of your life, Sean? The one your evil mother—"

"Yep."

"Well, girl, this is your chance to make it right. Kiss and make up." He leaned closer. "And, oh, believe me, the make-up sex can be"—he kissed his fingers—"*magnific*".

Never drink around Cary. She placed her drink on the nearest table to avoid the temptation of becoming intoxicated. She couldn't risk believing Cary's wild fairy tales. She'd known for years not to follow his advice, but until now she hadn't cared. Her heart thumped at the thought of being in her own fairy tale, but she was hardly heroine material. "Sean can't love me. *I* destroyed us, not my mom. So my feelings don't matter."

"Yes, they do." Cary stood up and went to the fire escape.

She followed, and Cary closed the window the second she had both feet on the metal railing. The cold night air had her body tingling.

Cary sat and patted the area next to him. "Come on, now."

With a sigh, she plopped herself down beside her good friend.

"Tell me what's going on, girly."

"Sean Collins bought the school yesterday."

"Did he know you worked there?" Cary sounded hopeful.

Nodding, she gently bit her lip.

"Is he working to win you back?"

"No. How could he? He never cared to look me up for months and I lived next door to him. He seemed shocked when he saw me." Sean had never pursued or chased her after she'd left. Of course she'd avoided him at every turn.

"Shocked is good. He followed you here to Paris?"

"Not followed, chaperoned. Sean's here for the school group, not for me."

Cary blew out an exaggerated breath. "Do I need to spell this out for you? He's a man and straight men are simple. He's here for you,"

Cary corrected.

A sense of calm serenity surrounded her, and her heart expanded. "Why are you not excited about this?"

"Why would I be? He hates me. He *has* to hate me. He wants to talk about the past."

"Ohh, that will be good for you both."

"I can't. I'll fall apart."

"So distract him."

"How?"

"Don't tell me you've forgotten."

She punched him in the arm.

"What? Is the chemistry gone?"

Despite the cool temperatures, her body grew warm again. "Well, we did kiss."

Cary squealed. "I knew it. I just knew it. Even all those years ago. Sean's the only man for you." His eyes narrowed. "So what's the problem?"

"I don't get why he kissed me or what I should do," she admitted.

"Funny girl. Do tell all."

"It was either kiss me or kill me," she repeated in a deep masculine voice. Then she whispered in her own voice, "His kiss tasted of summer moonlight and youth."

Cary poked her knees with his. "He *chose* to kiss you, little one. He's still attracted to you."

"He has every reason to hate me. I don't want to hear how he can never forgive me."

"Hmm. Evidence suggests otherwise. He kissed you. He followed you to Paris—"

"—to chaperone," she automatically finished. "He did ask me not to go on this, our, date."

"Wait, we're dating? Hmm, you'll have to rethink this," Cary said in a well-intentioned, best-friend way. Pushing her hip with his on the stair, he waited for her stare up at him then finished. "I'm not the best option to strike up the man's jealousy. So what's his life been like?"

"He has a son he's super proud of. His wife died before they finalized the divorce, and he battled cancer. All the cancer is gone now, and his doctors believe he'll be fine. At least he has his son, a reason to get up in the morning." She envisioned herself becoming mother to his son. *The Collins clan sticks together, through thick and thin,* his mother had once said to her.

"His life hasn't been easy then, yet he's richer than any other man I've known. The answer is staring you in the face, doll." Cary poked her.

She crinkled her nose. "What are you talking about?"

"First, in any kind of conflict resolution you have to get through the stormin' part before you get to the normin', well, in your case the screwin' part."

She gave him a horrified look. "What are you talking about?"

"You have to let him yell at you, Gigi. You ran away from home, and never giving him a right to say anything to you."

"No," she almost cried, and huffed a second. "I won't be able to take his anger." She shriveled her shoulders into her neck. "I can't."

"You can, and you will," Cary said firmly. He gave her a minute, then continued, his voice calming and sweet. "Words don't kill anyone. Then you convince him in time to forgive you. You kiss him, hold his hand, be there for him."

"I will?" Sean had taken her hand multiple times that day.

"Let yourself be happy, Gigi. You deserve a second chance. We all do. Then, of course, you show him a good time in bed," Cary finished with a satisfied grin. "You tell him you love him and then, boom, you both live happy-ever-after and invite me and the lucky hunk I'm dating to the wedding."

"Wow, that sounds so easy," she said in a state of shock.

"Little one, it's one conversation you fear. No one dies from talking, and you are an adult now. I've seen you tell people no," Cary told her.

She reached for her necklace. Sean *had* loved her once. "No other man ever compared to Sean, so there wasn't another option."

"Then trust yourself. Soon you get him to tell you he loves you." Cary said.

But happy ever after with Sean would be impossible.

"Little One, you can have Sean back if you put yourself out there."

How she wished everything would work out with a snap of her fingers and a little effort, but why should Sean believe her? Exhaling, she looked up at the full moon and stars. The moon, somehow, took the heaviness of her burden off her shoulders for that one moment. She closed her eyes, and pictured having a picnic with Sean off in the woods, near a babbling brook. Her life would be so different. But how to get from the here and now to the future? She opened her eyes.

Cary bumped his hip into hers. "Don't worry, doll. I'll help you win your man back."

"No." She shook her head, remembering running on the streets of Lyon covered in red paint because of one of his hair-brained schemes. "Your plans end in disaster."

"No, my plans always work. I get what I want. I had you move in and clean up after me for years. Now I need you to be a rich man's wife to pay for my alcohol. This will work."

"Ulterior motive, I see." She laughed then sobered as she touched him on the shoulder. "You know, Cary, you could come home. People are more tolerant these days, at least in many parts of our country."

"I can't. It's still too hard. My first love died there, remember?"

Tears prickled the backs of her eyes. Cary's lover had died of AIDS.

He playfully swatted her arm, "*I* never used Paris to *hide* from my true love. But I have found someone here, created a life for myself." He gestured toward the raucous party going on behind him. "Have you learned nothing from the French when it comes to love?"

She met Cary's eyes. He sounded sincere and he believed in fairy tales, despite the loss of his first love. She swallowed hard. "You're right. You don't always get a second chance. I will think about what you said, but you should know I don't believe in fairy tales anymore."

"Sweetheart, you're living in one. You have it in your power to decide the ending."

She trailed her fingers down her necklace to the ring. She remembered when Sean had put it on her finger. Maybe the heat exuding from her chest meant the future could be bright, too.

Sean wasn't sure exactly where in the world his brother Liam was, except for the fact he wasn't in Boston. They were both watching the Bruins game and they both screamed 'score' over the computer mic when the puck passed the goalie, into the net.

The yelling subsided, and Liam asked, "Let me get our conversation straight. You make me lots of money then want my permission to sex up Gigi again?"

"No." Sean clenched his teeth, knowing he hadn't said anything of the sort. He'd mentioned Gigi's name only. "I told you, Gigi's on a date with another man." *And I won't be touching her.*

"Lying to yourself about women is why you married Jennifer when no one liked her. Gigi's different on many levels," Liam admitted. "She's always been yours."

Sean thought about losing the connection to the Internet and this video call. Instead, he poured himself a glass of beer and nodded.

"Gigi's like my sister, though," Liam continued, "so it's always been kind of gross that my brother had a girl before I knew what the fair sex offered a man."

"She was mine. Once. But I have a family now."

"Reasonable," Liam answered. "But you want her back, because you still love her. You were always the sap. I say start with that line. Then remind her of what she lost. Don't let her go."

Making love to Gigi again had played in his mind all day, but he intended a long-term relationship. All those years ago, Gigi had run from him based on guilt, or at least his gut told him so. Sean held his glass in his hands then shrugged. "I have never been like you or Daniel. And I could never be like Gerard. I like women."

"We all like women. And none of us are at Gerard's level of cynical."

"Says the adrenaline junkie."

"Fair shot. But you and Gerard became our parents before you grew hair on your chest."

"I was responsible—"

"Ron?" Liam called to someone off screen.

Sean gulped his drink. On the viewscreen, a light flashed behind Liam near his window. Then he held the glass firm and asked, "Was that a bomb, bro? Where are you now?"

"I can't say, and they are actually fireworks. People are out celebrating." Liam turned back to the screen after staring off out his window. Sean didn't believe him. "So tell me what Gigi did to you that you are swearing off sex with her. Did she become a nun?"

"No, not a nun. She'd never qualify." Sean had never told anyone what had happened the night of Sean's birthday party except his mother, who'd seen him moping around and cornered him.

Sean gulped his drink. After that night, Gigi had kept her distance. He'd respect that choice. There'd been no alternative. "Doesn't matter. She ran off. Seriously, bro, I don't know if I would have bought the school if I'd known she came in the paperwork."

"You'd have bought it sooner."

"Let's change the topic. The game is on."

Liam laughed. "You brought that girl home and told Mom you had found your wife. If you can't have her long term, then bend her over the bed in every possible position and have your fill, baby bro. She's still under your skin, and, unlike Jennifer, we all like Gigi."

"I'll take your advice under consideration," Sean said, shaking his head at his brother's crude language. He'd correct him but history told him it'd do no good.

"Guess I'm getting my sister back," Liam said with a satisfied smile. "I did miss her opinions when she left. Guess we should have invited you into the clubhouse *before* you had sex."

"I'm younger than Daniel, Liam." Sean smiled. "And Gigi and I have both been in your clubhouse."

Liam stared at him with his mouth open. "*My* tree house? I knew Gerard snuck up. You, too?"

Sean laughed. "Daniel had come home all proud. Gerard dragged me up, listening to him brag to you about Caroline. But Gigi and I knew exactly what'd happened."

Liam scratched his son. "Caroline? Wait, yeah, I remember Caro. You and Gigi were freaks then?" Liam leaned closer to the screen. "Makes you sound more manly, bro. Like I said, I approve of her, even if she's not Irish."

"Ahh, but we'll have to get the church to give us a waiver to make Mom proud." Sean laughed.

Liam shook his head. "Yeah, your motherless child will need religion next. If I get a vote, Gigi is your best option. I'll run a background check to see if something happened to her in our database."

He hit a few buttons before Sean could get "Don't" out.

The sound of footsteps in the hotel's hallway caught Sean's attention. Could be one of the teenagers sneaking off, but the electrical energy in his body made him think *Gigi*. "I have to go, Liam. Talk to you soon. Go Bruins."

Sean clicked off the computer and rushed to his door. He blinked to force his mind to take in what he saw.

A half-naked Gigi stumbling down the hall with feathers in her hair.

Chapter 13

The next morning, Gigi woke up, ran a hand through her sticky hair, and groaned. Cary's party had gotten out of hand the only way one of Cary's parties could and, despite her best protests, she'd consumed some alcohol and did lots and lots of dancing.

And she hadn't had a good night's sleep. She rubbed her eyes and tossed in her bed. Every time she had heard a noise on the street, she had flinched. Last night in the hallway she had scurried into her room to avoid talking to Sean though she thought she'd heard a noise from next door. She groaned again then stirred to move.

Hobbling out of bed, she twisted the shower faucet on and brushed her teeth until the water got hot. She rubbed the back of her neck and told herself not to dawdle. Staring into the mirror, she noticed her eyes were red, contrasting sharply to her pinkish skin. The sleep deprivation must have stolen whatever glow people had mentioned yesterday. She turned away, showered, and then checked the temperature outside. As she paced, the prospect of facing Sean weighed heavily on her mind. Every cell in her body clung to the idea that she simply disappear and never speak to him again.

She licked her lips, remembering his kiss, then threw water onto her face.

At the door, she took one more whiff of herself. She inhaled. Damn. She still smelled of stale tobacco, and maybe something else, alcohol, and sweat. The shower hadn't cured everything. She shook her head. Cary sure knew how to party. Thankfully none of the students had seen her come in.

She washed with a towel one more time then brushed her teeth, again. Finally, she stopped smelling champagne. After throwing on a pair of jeans and a shirt, she glanced at the clock. Ugh, late. She let out a breath, and she rushed down the hallway. Silence greeted her. She marched to the girls' room and knocked on the door.

Kendra, still in her pajamas, half-opened the door then let out a yawn. "Ms. Dumont, we're sleeping."

Oh my god. The girls were in bed! Gigi swallowed but her shoulders tensed as she ordered, "If you want to see the city and practice, we have to stick to our schedule. Meet you downstairs in thirty minutes."

The other girls groaned and covered their heads with a pillow. Why wasn't anyone moving?

She repeated her message to the rest of the students then stared at Sean's door. Was he up? Should she knock? Her hands shook and her mind went dizzy, but she went up to his door and knocked. Softly at first then pounding with the side of her fist against the door. What if he answered the door in the same shirtless state as yesterday?

The second she heard the door rattling, she locked her knees in place to prevent her body from shaking. Her mouth fell open as he opened the door. Her heart raced. Yep, shirtless and sexy again. And where had those muscles come from? He motioned her inside, then closed the door. "Scout, you're the last person to be up. Why are you knocking on everyone's door?"

"How did you get a tan living in Cape Cod?" she blurted.

The weather hadn't been warm enough. His rock-hard body advertised sex and adventure. His muscles, chiseled from the molten fires of perfection, caught her every attention.

"Earth to Gigi." Sean waved his hand in front of her eyes, causing her to blink.

Her breathing quickened, and her lips parted. "It's nine A.M., Sean. We have to get going."

"Scout." He turned toward his bed of tangled sheets and directed her attention toward his digital alarm. He pointed and said, "No. It's *six* A.M. Nothing is open yet."

She stared at the red numbers in shock. That had to be wrong! How had she screwed up reading the time? "Oh no," she moaned. "I just woke the girls up."

The phone in his room rang. Sean held up his finger to ask her to be silent then answered. "Yeah, I know. I spoke to Ms. Dumont. She read her clock wrong. Go back to sleep. See you at nine." Sean yawned and hung up.

He raised his eyebrows at her. "I'm surprised at you. You had a late night."

"I couldn't sleep," her spine tingled and guilt tensed up her body.

"Guilty conscience?"

"No, Sean. I didn't do anything to be ashamed of." Well, maybe allowing Cary to don her with feathers had gone too far but Sean didn't need to know that. "Last night, I visited my old roommate. When I arrived, the party was in full swing. I wasn't—"

Sean shrugged and rubbed his head.

Her eyes narrowed as she watched him step closer to her. Trapped against the wall, she couldn't move. He lifted her elbow. "What are you looking at?" she asked, confused.

"You scratched up your arm. Were you climbing trees?"

"Don't be stupid, Sean. I'm not in the mood to joke at this hour of the morning." But she ached to reach out and caress his body. Her mind yelled at her to run. The indecision on her end must have looked like an invitation. Sean leaned closer, and took up every inch of space between them. She sighed, and her body electrified.

"What are you in the mood for?" he said in a seductive tone.

Without an answer, she licked her lips and met his hard stare, hoping her longing didn't show in her eyes. Finally, she softly answered, "Something I have no right to have."

Sean leaned down and kissed her. The sweet pressure made her tremble. "I shouldn't, but part of me wants you again, Gigi."

His lips made her forget everything.

Unable to stop herself, she wrapped her arms around his neck, and erasing any remaining space between them. Years of dreaming about Sean fueled her reaction, and she clutched his back. Her body slammed into the wall and her mouth never left his. She needed to have him.

Desperation on her end must have made him slow down. "Relax."

He picked up her leg and wrapped it around his waist. Then he kissed her and brought his body closer. Groaning, he lifted his head. "Good morning."

Ignoring every piece of advice she'd given herself over the past three days, Gigi reached for the zipper on Sean's jeans. She needed far more than a kiss. She had no right to forever, but she could have one moment today.

Sean's eyebrow quirked as he slipped her shirt over her head. To help, she unhooked her pink bra and tossed it across the room. A growl escaped her mouth then she grasped his hips to bring him back to her for another trail blazing kiss.

He trailed his hands lower on her body, and grabbed her buttocks. Her body softened and offered more. She swallowed and stared into his big blue eyes. He kissed her cheek, lightly brushed her mouth, then whispered a hair's breadth away from her lips. "Aren't we the chaperones?"

In-between gasps for breath, she said, "The teenagers are in their rooms. Sleeping." She kissed the side of his mouth, needing more than anything else to continue. She licked his skin, planting desperate kisses behind his neck, ears, and cheek until he deposited her on the bed.

"Gigi . . ." He kissed her neck, and she worked on her pants.

The feel of his body against hers amplified her desire to go faster.

He sighed. "We need to talk."

No. She couldn't talk. With their history and what she'd done, no. "We'll talk later, Sean, I promise. But I want you now." Trembling, she unbuttoned her jeans then unzipped his. She leaned forward, urging his lips to her mouth.

Sean spun off the bed and ran his hands through his hair. He shook his head. "We can't, Gigi."

Chapter 14

Gigi's shoes clanked on the marble floor in the lobby. Her body still trembled and as of last check, the blush on her face had never faded. Her chest tightened painfully. Sean had turned away from her and his rejection physically hurt.

How was she supposed to be a teacher today?

She sucked in a breath. The elevator doors opened and the girls giggled and stared at her when they stepped out into the lobby. The boys and Sean followed a short distance behind, and Sean's face held a reddish tint.

Great, they had a matching color.

Kendra, ever the bold leader, said, "Ms. Dumont, we're setting your alarm tonight."

"Fair enough. Sorry about this morning," Gigi responded, wondering what Sean could have possibly told the students. He had no reason to blush, but with that twinkle in his eye, she could only hope he respected the boundaries of a chaperone/student relationship. Deliberately avoiding Sean's gaze, she said, "Let's get breakfast. I'm starving."

"I'm sure you are," Kendra added slyly. Then, as if she couldn't restrain herself anymore, she said, "What were you doing in Mr. Collins' room?"

"I already told you. She stayed a short while to work and I played a video game," Sean replied, but kept his attention on her. "Ms. Dumont won."

"Yes. And I graded papers while Sea— Mr. Collins checked the stocks." Meeting Erika's gaze, she added, "Now we're going to get breakfast and see Notre Dame."

Erika opened her mouth as if to argue, then closed it again as she rushed to join the other students, already on their way to breakfast.

As Gigi met Sean's gaze, she felt like her cheeks were burning. OMG. She deserved to be fired. *Never corrupt other people's children* had always been a personal motto.

When Sean approached her, Gigi whispered, "Did they see or know anything?"

"Nothing happened, Geegs. You didn't answer your phone an hour ago when the girls called to check on you." He placed his palm against on her back, and fireworks exploded in her body. She fidgeted next to him, unsure what to do. "Relax," he encouraged. "If you don't, then they will suspect something."

They walked a short distance to a café for a pastry and coffee, and most of the teenagers discovered the hot chocolate tasted nothing like the powered stateside version. Here, hot chocolate consisted of a melted bar of chocolate inside warmed milk brewed slow and perfect. Every one of them of the students ordered the delectable concoction that morning. Sean ran his hand through his hair and signed. Then he took the seat beside her outside at one of the café tables.

When the students were occupied, Sean leaned over and whispered in her ear, "This morning you surprised me. We have a lot of things to talk about, but I don't know—"

"Wait." She gulped and kept her head low, knowing he still hated her. Then she whispered back, "Not here. Let's stay focused on our jobs right now."

He drank his coffee and stared at her. Was he trying to understand? Even now her muscles and nerve endings tingled where he'd just touched her. She'd likely float wherever they went today. Hopefully no one would notice.

Halfway through her breakfast, Gigi stopped eating and kept flinching anytime Sean brushed his arm against hers. She fumbled at her neckline and clutched her necklace.

She and Sean had no future. She cover her face with her hair and searched for something to say. "I can't wait to practice with my students today, and tomorrow is the dress rehearsal where they will have dinner with the Canadian and Chinese finalists. We have a real chance at winning."

"This afternoon I want to take them shopping," Sean said. She cleared her throat. "Shopping is not on the schedule or in our budget."

"France is known to be a fashion-forward place. My ex spent enough money here to convince me." He shrugged then added, "The six girls on your team will appreciate the gesture."

"Not all women are into shopping," she retorted.

"A dare?" He winked and called out, "Kendra, can you come here for a minute?"

"Yes, sir." Kendra filed over, with grace, but her gaze remained sharp and curious.

"I told your teacher I intended to buy the group outfits to wear for the competition. She doesn't think you'd appreciate shopping at Galeries Lafayette before you practice."

Kendra's face lit up brighter than the fourth of July. "Are you joking? Why would you do that? Oh, wait. I won't want a uniform."

"Not a uniform." Smiling his 'I told you so' smile, he continued. "I'm serious. I want my team to win, and if we have to ham it up to impress the French by wearing their clothes, I think it's smart. Will you take charge in ensuring everyone finds an outfit and help coordinate the choices in appearance?"

"You said you're buying, right?" The girl twirled around with glee.

"I'm buying," Sean answered. "Gigi laughed and the other students stared and watched Kendra dance, then she raced over to tell them. A few seconds later, screams of excitement caused everyone on the street to stop and stare them.

"Yes, yes, you win," Gigi said, meeting Sean's triumphant gaze. She took a sip of her coffee. "How do you know the name of places to shop?"

"I told you. The ex came here shopping. I know what stores took my credit cards and every dollar wasted." Sean shook his head. "I'm good at sticking to my bad choices."

Gigi flinched. Did he mean her, too? She crossed her arms. She stuck out her chin. "You're free now, so no more bad choices." She kept her voice light.

"I'd like a time machine to avoid them, but science hasn't figured it out yet."

"Can't have everything," she said, her voice cracking. "You can buy your seat on a space mission though. Counts for something."

Sean's voice hardened. "Not until my Patrick is grown. I hear the Mars mission will be seeking senior citizens to go. How's that for our retirement plan, Scout?"

"Sign me up." She hooted then glanced toward the students. "They'll love shopping. Should we cancel Notre Dame?"

"Let them run off some energy seeing a few places and buying souvenirs on their own. You and I can walk the Seine and watch them," he offered before finishing his pastry. "Then we go shopping."

He motioned for the check and withdrew his card.

Snatching up the bill, she reminded him, "We can pay for ourselves. You keep spending when we have our fundraising money."

Sean nodded and let everyone pay. He then gathered the students together and said, "Ms. Dumont said we're to ride the Paris Metro, and Raphael will tell us what train to get on and off to lead us."

The students' excitement reminded her why she loved her job. She checked the bill to ensure everything added up, and had a great view of Sean's butt. He turned around and her cheeks heated.

"Remember, my bother's in town tonight," he said as he approached the table.

She stood and put her hand on his elbow. "No worries. I'll watch the students tonight."

He tucked her arm under his and led her out of the café. She should have protested, but the birds singing back and forth from tree to tree caught her off guard. If only she hadn't ruined her almost family with Sean.

With Erica's help, Raphael led the group through the subway successfully. A spear of pride shot through Gigi. The students appeared to be understanding most everything. The boys had no issues reading the maps and deciding their exits.

Sean might not want her, but her life wasn't ruined. Still, she had to deal with the fact that she wanted him.

Chapter 15

Gigi had never wanted to spend much time in churches, but Notre Dame possessed such an awesome showcase of colors and beauty, especially their stained-glass windows. She could stay there forever and admire the beauty. She'd promised the students they could climb up the tower.

Tired from the night before, she decided she wouldn't go. Sean could supervise and her feet throbbed. Instead she took a seat in a pew, remembering Cary's advice. *Talk, let Sean spit out his anger, and then convince Sean to forgive her?* But when? She couldn't talk about this in front of the students and Sean was meeting his brother that night. And, more importantly, how?

Gigi blinked and stared at the religious artifacts. She'd never be able to pull off Cary's plan. Yesterday, Sean hadn't even wanted her with no strings attached. Her cheeks flamed. And she never threw herself at a man.

She clenched her hands together and released the heat building up inside her stomach. She shouldn't want him anyhow.

A family approached and sat in front of her, talking in hushed tones that their daughter would make her first communion here.

Gigi released her hands as she listened to the French family talk about the history of Notre Dame. The mother turned to Gigi. "Are you here for confession, dear?"

"No. You must be early. It's still open for the public."

"We are early, but you stared hard at the lovely stained glass with troubles floating in your eyes."

"That bad? It's nothing. My feet hurt. And I'm here with a school group," Gigi replied in French.

"American?" the woman asked, her mouth slightly open. "Your French is impeccable."

"I lived here a few years ago."

"But, forgive me, dear, you look upset. If this is a school trip, then why are you alone?"

Gigi sighed then shook her head. "They're up the tower. I'm resting."

"Whatever it is that's troubling you, let it go. Life is about renewal, not regret." The woman's easy smile and sly answer made Gigi's pulse thump in agreement. "Regret stops us from living."

Time stopped for a moment as Gigi contemplated what the woman had said. Was she right? *Could* she forgive herself?

If so, she'd fight for a chance at happiness.

A warm heat suddenly filled Gigi. Sean must have returned. So tuned into him to him now, her body responded even when he wasn't in sight. She turned around and stared at the door.

The woman dropped her sunglasses as they both glanced in Sean's direction. With a mischievous grin, she whispered, "If such a man is a regret, forgiveness will be heavenly."

Gigi had to agree. With sunlight shadowing Sean near the door, he looked like a dreamy Prince Charming. Her chest tightened. But she was no princess. Princesses were pure and innocent. And she was far from innocent.

"Geegs," Sean said as he approached, "I see you've made a friend." He gave the woman a warm smile. "The kids are waiting for us just outside."

"Okay." Gigi turned to the woman. Thank you for your advice."

Feeling suddenly lighter, Gigi followed Sean into the sunshine that whispered promises of love in paradise.

She reached into her bag and found her shades. Sean didn't move toward the students gathered nearby and instead stayed beside her. She felt her toes curling upward. Why did he still have such an effect on her after all these years?

Gigi waved the students ahead and she and Sean followed behind.

Sean leaned toward her. "We talked about days off, but I forgot. Tomorrow night is the evening cruise. Do you have any more plans?"

"Cary promised me a surprise, but if you need another night off, I'll stay."

Sean's chin pushed up higher at the mention her friend. Was Sean jealous? "Can I tell you about Cary?"

"What is there to know? You have a date."

"No, I don't." She rubbed her neck and found her necklace. Then she waited until she met his gaze. "Cary was my roommate. He's gay and would be attracted to you, not me. But I can't bring him to the hotel. He might show up as alter ego, Donna. We have some religious students on this trip, and it's not right to bring our personal lives into anything. Chaperones are supposed to be boring, sexless beings, and teachers are trolls who never leave their classrooms."

"Funny." Sean lowered his arm around her waist, and she could swear he sighed. She caught his gaze a few times, and his eyes grew bluer and stormy with emotions. He used to look at her like that.

Gigi swallowed. "I don't know what Cary has planned for me, but I do prefer keeping my personal life away from the students. I'm two different people. Not that I'm good or bad in either, but when teaching, students don't need to know your personal truths."

"Shh, Scout. You're sounding deep." He traced her hand, but held her arm with his free hand. "Thank you for telling me about your friend. I had been planning on killing him, but he gets to live now."

Kill Cary? Why? Her body grew hot. Could Sean still have feelings for her? She swallowed, unwilling to go *there* now. Playing it light, she said, "Sean Collins, you don't have a mean bone in your body, and we both know it.

"Besides, you and me, we're just old friends."

Sean made a strangled noise then went silent. Even with the sun, Gigi felt a sudden chill. They continued until they arrived at the fourth arrondissement that included Victor Hugo's home, the contemporary art of Pompidou, and the remaining stairs of the burned-down Bastille.

They students immediately found the small vendor stands with T-shirts and the students rushed there.

While she stood with her arms crossed, Sean texted someone.

After ten minutes of waiting for the students to finish up their purchases, Gigi guided them into Victor Hugo's home. Everyone's jaws dropped open as they took in the glass building with an airport-like tunnel guiding them upward.

They spend about half an hour absorbing the sights then left. Sean disappeared for a minute as they exited the museum then appeared a minute later and he returned and waved at the group. Four of the boys understood to join him. Gigi turned around and saw a shaded spot in the courtyard, where she led everyone.

A few minutes later, Sean and the four students returned with ice cream for everyone. The remaining teenagers gave cries of appreciation. Gigi smiled as Sean handed her a cup.

Sean winked. "Chocolate and vanilla mixed, in a cup not a cone. You never could decide."

"And I still prefer milk chocolate, not dark or white." She laughed and licked the spoon. "It's nice that you remember."

"Good. I always remembered you, Scout." He invited her to sit. The teenagers took their own tables a few spaces away. "We can wait here for the town cars to arrive."

"Two now?"

"One limo. Two cars. The limo is being used by some heiress named Kate Sparrow." Sean shrugged. "The two town cars will hold us."

"We can take the Metro again," she suggested, preferring them for an honest view of city life abroad.

"Shopping then practice," Sean reminded her. "With a car, no one loses a bag."

She brushed Sean's side and goosebumps formed on her forearms. She darted her gaze to the ground. For a minute, she lost her ability to think. She gulped, and shuffled on her feet. Then in a high-pitched voice, she asked, "Daniel is arriving while the students are practicing?"

"Yes. You'll be in the penthouse. I'll be in my room." Sean shrugged.

Her face heated. "Sounds good. When we get back, the students and I will eat a practical dinner on budget."

"Sounds boring." Sean's eyes gleamed. "Or Daniel can come to dinner with us. He asked about you when I told him who I came with."

"Daniel." Her chest squeezed. Had Sean told his family about what she'd done? She felt a tad bit faint. No. If Sean had told everyone, Daniel would never have asked about her.

The day she took off, she remembered Sean's mother had argued with her mother in their family kitchen. Gigi hadn't heard the words other than her name. She had been the subject of an intense argument. She had told Sean less than twenty-hours earlier what had happened, and she knew the Collins were a tight-knit family. Drawing a deep breath, she brushed her hair back and asked, "Did your mother say anything to your siblings?"

She met his gaze.

"Honestly, I don't know. I wasn't paying much attention but I don't think so."

Gigi ran her hand through her hair. "Still, I can't be sure.

For all I know, your brother probably hates me. I'd rather you two go off on your own."

"Daniel doesn't hate anyone, including you," Sean reassured her. "Don't worry about him. He's a doctor, out to fix everyone. And Liam likes you, too. He said you outclass Jennifer."

Gigi rolled her eyes. "Liam is still good with the back-sided compliments."

Sean smiled. "Now if Gerard visited, he would leave no stone untouched and quiz you until you break to find out why you left. But not Daniel."

Maybe Sean was right. Daniel had been the quietest of the Collins brood. Older than Sean, Daniel bore the responsibility of oldest child, but he'd always been a caregiver. "So how are Gerard, Liam, and your dad?"

"Gerard is never home. He's always in Boston," Sean answered. "Liam seeks out danger. And my dad hopes to retire, leaving the Collins Financial industry to me."

"You deserve it." Sean was the second oldest, but had always been the one after his father's approval. "You'll do a good job."

"Mom's happy." Sean licked his ice cream, and Gigi felt her face grow warm as she remembered his lips on her body, burning her skin. She almost dropped her own ice cream. "Liam worries me, Scout. He's chasing something or someone and isn't confiding in any of us." Sean kept his voice low. "I hope it's the job but something tell me it's more personal."

"You and yours will be there for him." If she had been born a Collins, her life would have turned out different. The Collins's stuck together, through thick and thin. "Does Patrick miss his mom?"

Sean crunched a bite of his cone. "I wish he didn't remember her at all. She told him she couldn't be his mother anymore. No child forgets that," Sean bitterly added then took another bite of his cone. "Patrick knows he has me, always, and he's a good boy."

"Patrick's got you and your mother." She gulped.

"She loves being a grandmother, though she still complains that she only has boys in the house and no women to watch romance movies with except the librarian."

"Sherry?" Gigi asked surprised. "Why, she's closer to our age than your mother's."

Sean shook his head. "I think my mother wants to set me up."

Gigi sucked in her breath then blew it out slowly.

Sean dropped his head to his side. "Thankfully Sherry doesn't seem to understand my mother's intentions."

"Ahh." Gigi clenched then unclenched her hand behind her back. *You have no right to be jealous, Gigi.* "I owe you a thank you."

Wrinkling her forehead wrinkled, she asked, "What?"

"A few months ago you found my boy." Sean ran a hand through his hair. "Patrick ran away. And I never said thank you for finding him."

"I was happy to help."

"Patrick hoped he'd bring his mother back," Sean said. "My ex told my son, her son, how he made her unhappy. Patrick's never gotten over that. Her hurting him is something I don't know how to fix."

Gigi covered her mouth with her hand and her eyes watered. She gulped and her heart ached for the boy. "And teaching your boy right and wrong is all up to you now."

"True," Sean added with a sharp tongue, though he patted her knee. "Jennifer can never hurt her again."

"So tell me about your cancer," she said, bringing up the subject she'd been long avoiding.

"I'm well. My blood work showed I'm in remission for a full year since last Thanksgiving. I have my appointment in March to check again, but the worst time was when I had the treatments and Jennifer kept riding the fence on leaving me. When she left, life became calmer."

"So you were able to heal in peace." She glanced at the students, saw they were occupied with each other, and rubbed his shoulder.

"Yes." He finished the last bit of his ice cream.

She cleaned up her cup and found a trashcan.

As the cars arrived, Sean motioned for everyone to pile into the vehicles. She called out, "Boys in the small one and girls in the big one."

She stepped forward to go with the girls and stared at Sean for a moment. In her life, he'd been the only man she ever counted on.

After the last girl's head disappeared into the vehicle, Gigi scooted in. Erica, on the seat next to her asked, "Why is Mr. Collins buying us clothes, Ms. Dumont? To impress you?"

"He wants to win the competition," Gigi assured her. "It's not about me."

"Yes, it is." Erica smiled. "You should go out with him. He likes you. You like him. We all agree."

"True," Kendra added in her opinionated tone. "Ms. Dumont, he's perfect for you, and he's hot, for an old guy. Makes me think of James Bond, only without the intense fight scenes."

"We're here to win the competition in three days, not to date."

"We can do both. Boys are cute and fun to talk about. If you want to attract Mr. Collins, though, you ought to consider buying more pinkish shades of makeup. You're light-toned, and the neutrals aren't good for you. We'll pick out a new outfit for you and a push-up bra. Men like those."

"And don't worry about Friday. We're going to win," Kendra added fiercely.

Before Gigi could respond, the town car stopped in front

of the department store. The girls' mouths dropped in unison as they stared at the fashionably dressed mannequins in the window fronts.

As they exited the car, Erica came up next to Gigi. "Wow. Do they allow American teenagers in?"

Gigi took the girl's hand and squeezed. "Of course."

The girls were spread out throughout the store when the boys' town car arrived. Gigi took charge and pointed Erica to a sales clerk, then waited near the entrance in the jewelry section, where she observed Sean's every gesture with the boys on what to look at and what articles to buy. Then he spoke to a salesclerk who joined him.

The boys followed the clerk, and Sean's eyes found hers. She smiled. He gave her the once-over and came toward her. Her face heated. She intended to place her hand on her hip to scold him, but she couldn't. So she laughed. Holding a straight face had taken too much effort.

Sean took her hand in his. "Can I buy you anything?"

"I appreciate the offer, but no."

He stepped closer, and she opened her mouth to protest, thinking he intended to kiss her but then he motioned for the salesclerk. "There is a hundred euro tip in it for you if you can talk Ms. Dumont here into buying anything."

Her mouth dropped. "That's not fair."

"Then you'll be the one depriving the girl of a tip. I have an errand to run." He handed Gigi his credit card and instructed her to buy the outfits for the students. "Be back as soon as I can."

He rushed off and she stared at his broad shoulders until she lost sight of him. Where the hell did he go?

Chapter 16

The town car doors opened and Sean breathed easier as the students grabbed their bags and entered his hotel like they were home. Gigi's car came to a stop as he shepherded his half of the crew up to their rooms.

Gigi's voice echoed in the halls as she called out, "You have five minutes to meet me upstairs to practice."

Sean let out his breath then raced to his room to ensure the place had no trace of Gigi anywhere. They hadn't gotten far in their make-out session but you never knew. With his heart racing, he threw open the door.

And heard his brother's laugh. Sean turned around and saw Daniel sitting in the living room reading. Daniel put his tablet to the side. "Who's the woman you had in here?"

"How do you know there was a woman?" Sean hoped his face hadn't turned red.

Daniel pointed to the nightstand and the pink bra.

Sean covered his face, then ran his hands down his side.

"So, bro, do you have another life you're hiding, and if so, we'll all accept you."

"Shut up." Sean shook his head. "Gigi surprised me."

"Things have progressed, I see." Daniel stood up and went toward the nightstand, then he raised his eyebrows. "Gigi Dumont? Again?"

"This isn't what you think. We're on a school function." How had he forgotten how he'd taken her bra off and thrown it?

"Gigi left you and broke your heart."

"I was young and stupid."

Daniel warned. "She hurt you once, bad."

"Tell me about it. And it was my fault anyhow. A few months before everything fell apart, I ripped the stupid condom in a rush. I was stupid."

Daniel shrugged. "And she could have told you her situation."

"I was there, remember?"

Daniel poked him. "So you want her back?"

Sean ran his hand through his hair. "I don't know. I don't know if I can forgive and forget what she did."

"No one said forget." Daniel answered. "But I think she was hurt, too. That girl practically lived at our house and never went home. I can't see her leaving like she did without being hurt."

Sean shook his head. "Doctor Daniel Collins. We're not all fixable."

Daniel shrugged. "Maybe I'm wrong, bro. I don't know. But I thought we agreed last month, you were going to date ten to twelve new women this year without getting serious."

"Neither of us are Gerard or Liam, Daniel." Sean sat down on the bed. "Thing is, what keeps bugging me is that Gigi's not Jennifer either."

"How? But Gigi left you."

"Jennifer was far worse. Gigi disappeared."

Sean body stayed straight as his brother asked, "Why?"

Sean sighed. Time to tell the truth. "Gigi was sixteen, about to turn seventeen when everything fell apart. Her life, my life, our life together ended." He blew out a breath, surprised how much it hurt after all these year. "While we were usually careful, she got pregnant. Her mother found out and forced her to have an abortion. She told me a week after her seventeenth birthday. At first I was furious but over the years, I've come to realize that we were both to blame for being young and stupid." Sean raked a hand through his hair. "But I'm having trouble forgiving her for leaving me."

"You need to talk to Gigi. This couldn't have been easy on her."

"I agree. You'll never mention it to her."

"No worries. How about we go out and take your mind of everything?"

In the hallway, Daniel admitted, "I was jealous of you and Gigi growing up. I was the oldest and you got the girl."

Sean nodded. "I thought Gigi and I would get married, have a family together." *It's not too late.* He shoved the thought aside and said,

"So what's the real reason you're setting up your practice near Hyannis."

"It's time to settle down."

The girl I was dating in Boston decided to plan the wedding only I haven't asked her. And I don't love her, not like Mom and Dad or you and Gigi."

"I said stop." Sean warned.

Daniel shrugged. "I'm not sure I want to move back to Hyannis port. I'm doing it because I don't know what else to do."

"Family is family, Daniel. You know that much." Sean smiled. "Every town needs good doctors and we can all vet out the crazy ones for you, Daniel."

The elevator dinged and Sean followed his big brother to go get a coffee and discuss women.

Gigi dragged out the practice until the students protested. Finally her students' whininess won, and she told them, "Great job. Help me clean up then we'll go to dinner."

"Finally," Kendra said but she picked up the soda cans near her.

Gigi supervised and soon the penthouse shined. With a nod, she let the students file out and called behind them, "Ten minutes then we meet in the lobby for dinner."

She gulped and hoped Daniel and Sean went somewhere alone. Her face heated at the thought of sitting with Sean's brother. If only she knew how much he was aware of what'd happened all those years ago. How her mother had forced her to do the unthinkable.

She locked the door behind her as sweat grew on her forehead.

"Gigi."

Sean.

Gigi gulped then turned around. Sean and Daniel sat right in the hall outside the penthouse. Her heartbeat raced. They were there. Why?

Both men stood

Daniel nodded hello. "It's good to see you again, Gigi."

"Wait." Kendra laughed. "Ms. Dumont's nickname is Gigi?"

Gigi's heart swelled as she heard Sean explain, "Ms. Dumont is an old family friend, but she's still your teacher."

"Yes, sir," Kendra said with laughter in her eyes. "And she was your ex-girlfriend. I get it now."

"Kendra," Gigi shouted in surprise.

A student learning her nickname wasn't the end of the world, but her relationship status went too far.

Gigi squared her shoulders then greeted Daniel with a warm smile. "It's good to see you again, Dr. Collins. What kind of medicine do you practice?"

"General medicine. I enjoyed the lymphatic system, but the benefits to own my own practice outweighed the specialization. You were always a *straight A* student, Ms. Dumont. You must rock at school being a cool teacher."

The students burst into laughter.

"As you can hear, I'm not exactly cool, Daniel. But I did get there here. Now let's all head to dinner."

She led the group downstairs. A few minutes later, they arrived at a restaurant that overlooked the Champ Elysee.

At dinner, the students sat at one long table. Her heart fluttered a bit. But she, Sean, and Daniel took the table next to them and the door, but the set-up gave them some privacy. Gigi gazed at the two brothers who shared a smile.

Gigi dropped her head and hoped she didn't blush. She had always loved the Collins's.

"So," Gigi said, "how is life treating you, Mr. Fancy Doctor?"

"I am staying at a place in Boston. It's different in the city. Everyone rushes around, and opinions are serious minded matters but no one stops to chat about their day. The hot zone where I spent the last two years, bandaging up soldiers . . . it hasn't hit me yet." He paused. "I am considering going home to Cape Cod."

"Hyannis is where you belong." Sean turned the tables on his brother. "And Gigi can help find you a woman or we can stick mom on that task."

"Mom? No," Daniel answered fast. "I'm buying a house, but I'm not sure I'll ever settle down fully. I'm happy being single."

The terseness of his answer stopped Gigi short. She smiled and remembered his poker tell. "There was a woman recently."

Sean and Daniel's eyes both opened wide, Sean's, in excitement for sharing and Daniel's, in shock. Gigi winked at Sean, just like when they were twelve and playing a game against his brothers.

Sean smiled at her and her heart grew. Maybe they had a chance.

"How did you know?" Daniel asked, tilting his head. "And she turned out to be crazy. I dated her for a month, and she was planning the wedding."

Gigi smiled victoriously. "If you thought of me as your sister once upon a time, then you were my brother. And Sean was my pretend husband. I remember your taste went to the quiet ones, though your mother is not quiet."

"Quiet can mean still waters, Geegs." Sean's hand squeezed her leg.

She stared at him for a minute and lost her train of thought.

"She called the hotel already," Daniel said sheepishly.

"Intriguing." Sean added for measure, "Gigi's volunteering to find you a date."

"I'll find Daniel a good woman, though she won't be quiet." Gigi thought hard. Most of the women in Hyannis wouldn't work at all. Daniel needed a woman with fire, but helping the Collins family spelled out fun. And her pulse soared.

With a flick of her ear, Gigi signaled Sean to let Daniel off the hook and not push for more.

Sean winked back and added, "Daniel has no idea what's in store."

Gigi laughed. "Don't worry, Daniel, we'll find you a woman when we get home."

With a mischievous expression, Daniel turned to Sean. "And what about you, bro? Gotta get you a woman, too."

Sean's heated gaze met hers. "I think I've already found one."

Chapter 17

Ten minutes after arriving at her hotel room, Gigi heard a knock at her door at her door.

Her body froze and she had difficulty breathing. She remained on the chair, unmoving.

The knocking continued until her ears drummed. Ignoring him wasn't the answer. Finally she got up and opened the door.

Sean stood there, and she backed up, unsure what to say.

Sean stepped forward. Darn, he really was standing in her hotel room. And she was awkward and unsure now.

"Gigi, can we talk?"

"No," she mumbled. She knew exactly what he wanted to talk about and she'd had to great a day to bring *that* up. No, she had a better idea on how to distract Sean. Keeping her eyes pinned to his baby blues, she unbuttoned her shirt and lifted it slowly over her head.

"No." She noted that Sean's breathing had become labored, and she placed her hand on his hip, and curled upward to kiss him. "We need to talk. Why did you never call me?"

"You deserved the fairy tale life."

"Stop. You left and I fell for Jennifer. She swooped in and caused tension and drama in my family."

"You're so smart. How did that happen?"

"I only knew you. Everyone else learns their mistakes early, but I spent my childhood with you."

"Stop." She stepped backward. "I didn't marry you to anyone. I left."

"Yes, you did." A fraction of an inch from her mouth, he stepped away from her and all she had was a fast, unexpected peck. He ran his hands through his hair. "As tempting as you are, I'll have to take a rain check, Geegs. We have to talk. Now. Before any more time passes."

Heart pounding, she automatically clutched her necklace.

He sighed. "I can see I've upset you but in order to move forward, we need to talk."

"No. I can't. I don't want to talk. You should go."

"We used to talk all the time, Gigi. Then you left, never speaking to me again. No notes, nothing." Sean dug his hands into his pants pockets and stepped back. "You disappeared on me."

She stepped back and left a wide space between them. Then she clasped her hands together to keep her hands from shaking. Sucking in her breath, she said, "I can't."

"Yes you can, Gigi. We *have* to. Don't you see?"

Her throat constricted, and she shook her head as tears pricked the backs of her eyes. She turned away, fighting against the unshed tears.

She intended to stay quiet and kept her mouth shut. Then she swallowed, and without prompting, her lips moved and the floodgates opened. "Mom figured out I was pregnant before I did. After conversing with the doctor, she took me home and locked me in my room for the night without my phone or computer or anything to call with. The next morning, she took me back to the doctor and gave the orders. When they asked for my approval, I didn't know what else to say." She tore her gaze from Sean, and stared at the open window to the night sky. "Agreeing destroyed me."

Sean stepped closer. She smelled his delicious smell of home. "I waited years. I thought I hated you, yet when you told me just now, I believed every word. You should have told me."

"So? Why do you want to talk now?" She held back tears.

"Gigi, I loved you." Tears refused to stop leaking despite her best efforts. This was going so wrong. "Stop. We can't. Just go."

Sean stepped closer. "I need to know . . ."

"Why I told you I had an abortion right before I blew out my birthday candles?" Tears fell freely now. She brushed his hand off her shoulder and turned to face him. "You shouldn't want me. I needed you to hate me then. I needed to forget what I did. I hated me, and you should have too."

"Sweetheart, holding on to pain only makes us lonely, sad individuals."

She stared into his warm blue eyes and her throat constricted. Finally, she told him, "I could have figured everything out sooner. It took me years to and to carve out a life for myself . . ." She paused and lowered her voice. "You don't understand, Sean. I'm so afraid."

"Of what, Geegs?"

"That I'll turn out just like her."

He shook his head, "You've never been like her. And don't tell me you don't care about me." "Stop." Her mother pushed people, not caring and getting her thoughts in. "I can't."

"Can you really forgive and forget, Sean?"

"No."

She bit her bottom lip. "Right, and you and your son deserve more. I hate sounding like this whiny, crying person I am right now. I'm not this girl anymore. And I can't go backward. Just go back to your room."

He took a step toward her, but she stepped backward. He dropped his hands to his sides. She couldn't breathe. "I need to know one thing, and I won't darken your door again."

"What?"

"Did you ever love me?"

Her shoulders caved in and she fought back tears in her eyes. "Once upon a time, I loved you more than life itself.

I'd have done anything for you, and by staying away from you all those years, I helped you far more than you realize."

"That doesn't make any sense." His intense blue eyes struck her as being both haunted and strong. She swallowed her tears that never formed as he finished his question. "Don't I get an opinion?"

She rolled her shoulders back and stared at him straight in his eyes. "Did you hate me when I left?"

"Yes."

Calmness enveloped her. "Then I did what I was best."

He stood still. "I can't argue about the past. What's done is done. Do I get a say in our lives, or are you making the decisions?"

Then he took her hand and placed his free hand on top of her hand. "I almost died, and now I see how I wasted too much energy being with the wrong people and unhappy."

The calmness dissipated and she shook. "I hurt me. I hurt you. I kept my mouth shut and did what I was told. Don't you see? I did what my mother wanted instead of running. I froze." Tears fell on her cheeks again. "Please, Sean, go."

He stepped away from her. "Fine, but this isn't over."

She pushed him out the door, and closed it behind her fast.

They had four more days to go. She twisted to look out at the night sky then at the Champ Elysee. She heard a saxophone in the distance. For some reason, the sweetness made everything worse.

Chapter 18

Sean's hands remained fisted as he paced his room. He should have known better. He stormed in a circle, his blood hot What had happened? Then his gaze stared at her bra and he dropped his hands to his sides in a loud sigh.

The walls seemed too narrow. Staying here wouldn't help him. His mind swirled around one fact. All those years ago, Gigi Dumont hadn't loved him like he had her. And now, some cruel twist of fate had her back in his life again.

He clenched his fists and wished for a fight. Like before, Gigi had snuck past his defenses. He was a prize idiot, and now he needed a hard drink. Not that he could have that right now. He threw water on his face and stared into the mirror. What could he do? He had no way of getting her to listen.

Gigi Dumont. He left his room and walked downstairs to go to the gym. At the elevator he stared at the numbers. What had he done to her? He walked into the empty elevator and went downstairs to the first floor. Everything had been fine, and then she'd gotten pregnant, aborted his child, then left.

The doors opened and he proceeded to the gym. A moment later, he hit the bag hard.

The past flashed in his eyes and he hated Lillian even more than he had. Gigi's mother had hated him since his sixteenth birthday. And Lillian had taken her revenge.

He punched the bag a few times.

Gigi hadn't trusted him or cared. He beat the bag a few more times.

Later, he wiped the sweat from his brow, and he stared at

the blood on his hands. He should have worn gloves, but he had no pain. Numbness filled his body.

At least he had worked out the pressure on his shoulders.

He grabbed his shirt, tugged it on, and headed straight to the bar. One drink would not leave him hung over and Gigi was on call this night.

A patron wrinkled his nose at Sean's hand, but the man and his lady friend were welcome to leave his hotel if he offended them. The bartender must have agreed since he didn't say a word, and simply asked, "What are you having?"

"Whiskey." He needed something hard to burn away his embarrassment. Gigi had a right not to love him, and he needed to not want impossible women.

The bartender was fast with his drink order. Sean sighed, took a sip, then closed his eyes.

Today did not end as he'd imagined.

Then he opened his eyes and took another sip. His mind kept asking the same question. How would he survive four more days with Gigi Dumont?

Chapter 19

Without an ounce of energy, Gigi dressed in a nice pink dress. A dress was required for entering a few churches in France and the schedule held they would visit Sacre Couer today. She tied her unruly brown hair back with a ribbon and decided she appeared good enough for Versailles. Black wasn't an option. She squared her shoulders. She'd have to face Sean Collins and somehow build a bridge to keep the peace for the rest of the week.

She stepped outside and stopped. Shouts in the hall were never good. Without buckling her other shoe, Gigi raced down the hall.

The girls' door was wide open and they all appeared to be screaming at one another.

Great! Just great.

At least no one looked hurt. Gigi took in a breath, then asked Erica, "What happened?"

"We don't know. David had a black eye."

Gigi looked around. But David wasn't there.

Kendra shook her head.

"He's not here. Mr. Collins took him and the other boys back to their room."

"The boys were here?" Gigi asked, shocked. As their faces darkened in embarrassment, Gigi had her answer. Not the one she wanted but the truth. "Go get dressed. We'll get a breakfast soon, and I'll straightened everything out."

At Kendra's soft sob, Gigi touched her shoulder. "A black eye will heal."

"It could be he didn't take his medication last night, Miss Dumont." A tear slid down Kendra's cheek.

"No one hit him?"

"I don't think so," Kendra admitted.

Damn. How had she forgotten to make sure he'd gotten his pills. But Sean had passed out all the meds last night, hadn't he? What a dolt she was.

If the boy needed a hospital, she'd bear the blame. She knocked on the boys' door and proceeded inside. Her heartbeat calmed at the scene before her. Sean had control of the situation. David's medication sat next to him.

"Do you need me to call his parents?" Gigi asked.

Sean's gaze shot up at her. "I have Raphael on the line with them now. The boys swear he fell. David seemed to have some trouble breathing. The paramedics will be up in a moment."

Sean remained calm and collected. And she trusted him. He understood cancer and had this under control. "You wait with David, and I'll get the rest of the students on our way. Call me with news."

"Good idea. Go. And don't worry."

Gigi took the other three boys, then went down the hall and knocked on the girls' room and told Kendra the update. Soon they were all gathered in the lobby. At the door, she reminded everyone, "David will be fine, everyone. Let's give him space, and he'll meet us there."

She swallowed her guilty conscience. Sean had to have made sure David had taken his pill. She couldn't have remembered wrong.

"What about breakfast, Ms. Dumont? You said we were going to the café."

"Yes, there is awesome food near Versailles."

"What if David needs one of us?" Kendra asked, her voice trembling.

"His parents are on the phone, and Mr. Collins is with

him." Gigi smiled at the girl to assure her. "He'll be fine. He's alert and conscious. He'll be happy you're enjoying yourself."

"But I want him with me all the time," Kendra wailed.

"Men need to see we're independent and can live without them," Gigi said, answering from her heart.

"Ms. Dumont, you don't understand love."

Boom. How true was that? Gigi wondered.

Kendra lagged behind the group Mimi led to the Paris Metro. Every few minutes Gigi checked her phone. No messages appeared.

Her shoulders stayed squared. When they arrived at the station to take the Versailles line, she texted Sean asking for the status. A few seconds later, Gigi read the report and told everyone, "David's fine. The doctor on call told him to eat a full breakfast, rest for a couple hours, and he should be strong enough to go out again."

Gigi felt her shoulders relax. The group continued onto the next train in a happier mood. She straightened and vowed to remain calm, no matter what. The students needed her, and she needed to be strong and good enough.

At the station, Kendra marched the group from the front. Gigi's smile grew. Slowing near Versailles, Erica asked Kendra, "How do you know where to go?"

"The signs." Kendra's natural leadership skills emerged and she took control again. "You should be reading them."

Gigi nodded. Good. Kendra had been the group's unofficial queen bee, and she returned to form. If they won in three days, she would complete this journey on an upswing. Sean or no Sean.

Liar.

After a full meal, the group finished the short walk and entered Versailles, where Gigi couldn't imagine life at the French Court. How strange the French kings lived. And so far removed from reality. The students were looking in all different directions. "You have your cell phones?" Gigi asked.

All the heads bobbed up and down.

"Good. You have two hours. I'll meet you at the reflecting pool."

Everyone paired off while she wandered over to the Petite Palace where Marie Antoinette had lived. The French Queen had had a strange pampered, but tutored life.

The palace had quiet gardens most tourists ignored. Gigi checked her backpack and tapped her reader. She intended to sit and catch up on a book. She found a shady spot and immersed herself in the story.

She had no idea how long she sat, but her body heat index rose higher and higher without the text being quite that interesting to elicit a visceral response. She rubbed her neck and stopped reading. Only one person could cause such a reaction. She scanned her surroundings. Only a tour group stood nearby.

"In 1760 . . .

"a tour guide started but she didn't pay any further attention.

Gigi trudged forward, hoping to glean some new information she could pass on to the students.

Her body swamped with sudden heat. "Sean, come out where I can see you."

Then, near the largest window frame, she saw him. Tilting her head, she asked, "What's going on? Why are you here?"

Staring at the interplay of shadow and sunlight on his frame, she lost her ability to speak. Sean faced her, and her body longed for him. He stepped inside the opulent room, and his fingers traced her body. She sighed, and he pulled her closer. He smelled like home again.

She took a whiff and then moistened her lips to ask, "What's going on? What's happening?"

"I have a new plan with you."

His words made her heart race.

Her body's overheating with need weakened her defenses. "What's your plan?"

"I decided I want you."

She pushed back in his arms. "Wait."

"What now?"

She stopped struggling. "Did you tell David to take his pills last night?"

"Yeah."

Relief washed through her. At least David's accident wasn't due to negligence on either of their pasts. Sean leaned closer to her, leaving no air except the shared space between them.

She licked her lips in anticipation.

Finally, he ended the torture and kissed her.

His lips lit a match inside her, and her need for him grew.

Sean twirled her to the window seat, pushed her backward, and tasted her neck and skin. His salty taste left her breathless.

Gigi almost jumped out of her skin. Her body became engulfed with intense heat and she had no defense. Her body quivered from a mere taste of him.

Sean had power over her but she didn't care. She her hand ran through his hair, wanting more of him. She'd never forget him.

She waited long enough, and her arm encircled his back. She needed him closer.

Chapter 20

Gigi's phone vibrated in her back pocket. Her fingers stayed in Sean's hair, then the ringing grew louder.

With a heavy sigh, she withdrew her cell phone. Sean's kiss had given her energy, but duty remained first.

Sean stepped back.

She stared at the caller ID and said, "One of the girls."

"Erica's run off crying," Kendra said.

"Where are you?" Gigi heard the answer and finished, "Be right there."

"One of the girls needs me." She propelled out of her seat, but her hormones off kept her unsteady on her feet.

"Why did you kiss me?" she asked as he kept pace by her side.

"I have a new plan regarding you and me, Gigi." Sean winked at her.

She swallowed and she imagined herself needy and weak, waiting for him on his bed. Something shifted inside her as she pictured them making love, as they had all those years ago. She shook off the visual and raced out of the house.

First, she had work to do.

Running hard and fast, Gigi focused on the task at hand and found Erica curled up with her knees to her chest on a park bench a short distance away. Catching her breath, she approached the girl and took the seat at the other end of the bench. "Are you okay, sweetie?"

"No, but I will be once people leave me alone for a while," Erica answered, staunch and firm. At least no tears were being shed.

"I can't help you if I don't know what happened," Gigi offered. "Mr. Collins, can you go find the others for me?"

Erica waited for Sean to leave then admitted to Gigi, "I overheard Raphael talking to David. They didn't know I was there, and you can't tell them," Erica said softly.

"Sure," Gigi assured her. "What did you hear?"

"I'm a nice girl, but plain and ordinary."

"Ouch," Gigi said.

"Teenage boys can be stupid, but they honestly don't know better."

Erica crossed her arms. "They should. I want to transform myself into one of the cool girls, like Kendra, or put on leather pants to get noticed."

Gigi scooted closer to her. "Don't do that. Transforming yourself into someone else denies who you are or what you want. Things happen in this world that we don't want to happen, and events force us to change into people we don't like sometimes. To change on purpose for someone else denies you your own destiny."

"Did Mr. Collins do that to you?" Erica gave her an assessing look. "Unlike Raphael, you should forgive him."

Gigi shook her head. "What happened wasn't Mr. Collins' fault. I'm the one that changed, no matter how much I didn't want to."

"Ms. Dumont, that's the stupidest thing you've ever said."

"What?"

"Nothing or no one can change who you are on the inside except you. All I want to do is change my clothes, to look pretty like Kendra. I won't be changing 'the me' on the inside. I am unchangeable, and so are you. You're a good person, Ms. Dumont."

Gigi paused. Erica had a point about being strong on the inside. "Do you want to ask Kendra for clothes and makeup help? She'd probably agree."

Launching off the bench, the girl shouted, "Great idea. Thanks. I'll go find her."

Gigi stilled for a moment and stared as the girl bounded off.

One again, with warning, goosebumps rose on her. The special goosebumps caused only by one person. Then, in the far right-corner near some rose bushes, she spotted Sean watching her. Anticipation built inside her, and her mouth watered to kiss him.

Then a cold, sobering thought hit her. Sean needed to find a woman capable of loving him heart and soul.

With hesitation, she forced herself to amble toward him. Should she look for a woman for Sean?

She'd go with a free conscience. Freedom might be lonely, but it was best for Sean.

Unaware of her thoughts, Sean walked over with his hands in his pockets and asked, "What was wrong?"

"Girl stuff. Clothes. You wouldn't understand." She answered Sean in a happy tone. He smelled good, fresh, linen mixed with almonds.

"Women troubles. I fall into that, no matter what I do." He winked at her, and scooted closer to nudge her. "I'm so thankful every day I have a son. Daughters are far too dangerous."

Add a great mother to the list she'd create on the perfect woman for Sean. She also had to appreciate his good qualities. If she made him happy, her would be at peace.

"You're looking at me funny," he whispered into her ear.

Growling, she admitted, "I am."

"Hmm." Sean took his hands out of his pocket. "What's your new plan, Scout?"

"I'll tell you later." She opened her mouth to add something, but he caught her lips in a fast kiss.

The world spun. She clung to him, and he became the center of her universe. Nothing else mattered.

Her fingers tugged on his back, and he let her go. But he kissed her forehead, and promised, "Scout, you are going to give us another change."

No. He had everything upside down. She'd never be his.

Without a word, he grabbed her hand and directed her toward the reflecting pool. Washington DC's reflecting pool in front of the Lincoln Memorial was a direct replica of Versailles. She and Sean had visited that on their eighth grade field trip together. Nearing the water, he twirled her around. She laughed despite her worry.

He wrapped his arm around her waist. She stopped mid-stride and her body heat index grew. Then with a grin he took her other hand and changed them both in a dance pose. A giggle emerged from her. "What are you doing, Sean?"

"Reminding you what you forced me to learn." He guided her body into the dance.

Waltzing in broad daylight made her laugh. "I preferred dancing to battling you in tackle football."

"You played me twice a week," he reminded her.

"You won every game, but I won a dance. To me, the games were fun." She laughed, and remembered how important she'd considered herself back in high school.

Sean Collins had loved her and had kept her close. Nothing else had mattered.

Life before she ruined everything had been idyllic with Sean. He'd made her forget her home life and dream of a possible future together, one far away from her uncaring mother.

Sean twirled her around, then unexpectedly swung her into a low dip.

Claps rang out.

Gigi knew her cheeks were tinged with red.

Raphael called out, "Mr. Collins, men don't dance fancy like on television. Stop. You're embarrassing our kind."

Gigi dropped her hands, then almost fell out of Sean's arms. Sean caught her, and protected her. Just like he always had.

"Wrong. Don't stop." Kendra said with her brow crinkled and her arms crossed. "David *will* learn how to dance if he plans on taking me to the prom. If you want a woman, you better know how to dance."

"She'll dance salsa. I'm Cuban and Puerto Rican," Raphael countered.

"Ms. Dumont needed a dance," Sean called, mischief dancing in his blue eyes. "So, are we hungry for lunch now?"

Cheers of *yes* echoed in her ears, but her thoughts stayed with him. Sean pointed in the direction of the crowd then took her hand.

She stayed back, his gaze flashed toward her. He slowed his pace as the group left. He neared her and she whispered, "Sean, I don't know what your plan is, but—"

Thud.

He had turned around, and let her walk straight into his arms without her even realizing it. He kept his arms on her back and whispered, "My plan is seduction, Scout. The thing you wanted to do to me last night."

Her entire body heated. She hadn't expected his blunt answer, though she could feel a huge smile spread across her face. "Sean, I can't marry you."

"I didn't ask you to." His fingers traced the outline of her spine, creating a tingling sensation on her body.

"I'm afraid we're going to have to table this, uh, discussion. Right now we're going to act like responsible adults."

Sean moved fast and she almost fell forward. Then he stepped out of her way. His hands steadied her, then held her. The teenagers hadn't seemed to notice. Instead the teenagers sat down, ordered sodas, and talked about winning the competition, and she and Sean took a second table. She ordered a bottle of water.

She kept her gaze on Sean and, finally, the waiter returned and Gigi gulped down the cool drink.

Sean stayed in his chair next to her, picked up her bottle, and poured himself a glass. She stared at his every move. "You and I, this whatever it is between us will burn out fast."

"Who are you talking to?" Sean asked her. "You've never left my heart, even if you did disappear for a decade. You're still there, Scout."

"That's not good." But how did she argue with him when her heart soared? He'd been her one true love.

"Then tell me you don't love me."

"It's not important." She had always loved him. The fluttering in her stomach from his every touch couldn't be stopped. And he'd never know. "What matters the most to me is you're happy."

"Glad we agree on one thing." Laughing, he drank his glass of water, and she clutched her bottle. Then she let it go. He wanted more from her than just water. She needed to convince him she would be the worst possible candidate for a wife and mother to his son. Why did she have trouble controlling her heart now? He put his empty glass down. "I agree with you on one thing. I should be happy. And so should you."

She cleared her throat and dizziness threatened to take over. "Sean, you need to let me go."

"After you stop confusing me with your mother. We don't look alike. I'm much cuter. You tell me you don't love me and I'll leave you alone." He leaned closer, fixing a piece of her hair. "Your mother did this to us, and despite everything, you can't say no to me."

Gigi watched as Sean sat back and glanced at the menu. How would she get through today and stick to her plan? But was Sean right? Could she be one for him?

Chapter 21

Sean kept his gaze on Gigi, realizing he was no longer angry at her. The past was the past, and he had a second chance at life. No cancer. No Jennifer. But Gigi still held the flames in his heart. Flames that now grew wildly. His new plan must work, or tonight he'd buy boxing gloves.

The tour stopped at Sacre Couer and the teenagers and Gigi climbed out of the bus. Soon, they followed the crowd and climbed the tower. Sean kept back to read what his brother reported. He'd then find Gigi for a candle ceremony.

His new plan would help her forget the past.

Earlier that morning, when David had talked to his oncologist, Sean had experienced his first epiphany. He had never claimed to be the inspired, creative type, but he realized that Gigi still held on to the past. She'd never mourned what'd happened to both of them. All their losses. When his grandfather had died, the mass had been solemn and hard. Afterward, though, remembering his granddad had become easier.

And after he completed his plan, he'd keep tossing grenades of truth, love, and desire in her path until she either exploded at him or explained herself. Direct confrontation became the most direct route to victory.

Soon his life would be back on track.

He read the text from Liam.

Gerard and I will call you tonight about a case we worked together five years ago. We tried to tell you the day you married Jennifer.

Odd. No memories surfaced where his brothers had not talked to him candidly. He remembered his brothers telling him not to marry Jennifer.

They'd even argued with him ten minutes before the wedding ceremony.

Sean stared at his phone and scratched his neck.

Years ago, Gerard had said something strange about sex changing a woman. Liam had said something about women taking after their mothers. But no one had mentioned Gigi. Sean remembered those comments because they stuck out as strange.

He put his phone in his pocket then sped up to rejoin the group. Sean caught the tail end of the tour guide who explained to the group how the French Revolution split the political and religious classes into different factions. The students' *ahs* made the exercise worth the trip.

Gigi surprised him and she stood next to him. She brushed against his hand and said, "This is still amazing. I never came here when I lived here."

"On and off for ten years, and you skipped one of the best views in the city?"

"As you might imagine, Churches weren't on my radar, no."

"I'm sorry things were so hard for you. I know now that you were all alone. I at least had my family." He took her hand in his and squeezed, and this time she didn't run away. Instead, her smile beamed from her face, making her beautiful.

Now. He quietly led her to a small candlelit area.

Her eyes narrowed. "What's this?"

"When we were children, you wanted an outdoor wedding and you never wanted your mother invited." Sean hadn't been sure how to phrase his question and the statement plopped out. Gigi stared at the altar. Nodding, he bowed his head. "I hoped you'd indulge me in lighting a candle in memory of that child, our child, that we were never able to have."

"What?" She stepped back, her body stiff and frozen. "But, Sean, you know me. I've never been religious."

Sean kept his hands to his sides and stared into her brown eyes. "You weren't hiding from me, then. Gigi, whatever your mother did to you, it's done. She's dead and can't hurt you anymore." He picked up the elongated wooden matches. "This is for us. To remember."

"Sean, the students." Her eyes widened. "We can't do this here."

""The students are busy at the moment. Please, let's do this together. We need to mourn to move on."

She hesitated a moment, then her fingers met his on the match. Her eyes stayed closed for a long while until she blinked a few time, and met his gaze. "Okay."

He let her take the match to the candle, and his hand found a place to touch her on her upper arm. She solemnly lit the candle. "For what might have been," she said softly.

"For what still may be," he said as he ran a finger along the top of her hand.

He leaned closer and whispered in her ear, "Once upon a time, you trusted me to help you. I can't pretend to understand anything or give up anything until you remember that I've always been there for you."

She stepped away from the altar and pretended to be interested in a delicate statue of a young girl. "But thank you for this. I stopped letting myself care of what might have been our future. You're right. I never took the time to mourn."

"You're stronger than you give yourself credit for, Gigi. You have students who adore you and your strength, but this time you need to fight for you."

Nodding, she stared at the candle a few more minutes. He waited until she was ready then led her back to the tour. No one had even noticed them gone.

A short while later, the bus returned them all back to the hotel.

Gigi stayed near him, but told everyone in the lobby, "Now we practice."

He listened to her for a few minutes strategizing with the students on how to be successful on stage. The group then went to the penthouse.

Sean held back, and at his first chance, he went back to his room to call his brother Gerard. Liam's text still struck him odd. Sean attached his phone to the television for the video conversation.

On the second ring, Gerard's face appeared. "Hey, bro, you're in."

"Sean, wow. Good timing. I need to talk to you."

The seriousness in Gerard's tone put Sean's question on hold. "What's happening?"

"You're in Paris with Gigi Dumont?" Gerard asked.

"Yeah. I want to ask you—"

"Wait," Gerard interrupted. "You bought the school she works at?"

"Yeah, it's the one I worked at. Why?"

"Someone filed a charge that you hired a hitman in Los Angeles, had Jennifer followed and killed before she boarded that plane to Tibet."

"What? That's insane." Sean felt his mouth drop open, and he squeezed his eyes shut. That was the year he'd battled cancer in Boston and he'd spent the year recovering on the Cape. No one could possibly believe that.

"I know, it's stupid and I'm already on this, bro. Don't worry, but the papers are drawing conclusions."

"Strange." A sickening rush of adrenaline coursed through Sean. Jennifer, somehow, had struck back at him from beyond the grave.

Then a memory flashed in his mind of when he'd told her he had cancer. She'd blamed his disease on his still obsessing over his baby-killing ex-girlfriend. How he wished he'd never told her but Jennifer had been his wife and at the time he'd trusted her. "Why did you bring up Gigi?"

"Two reasons. In the complaint, she's listed as your motivation."

Sean shook his head. This made no sense. "I hadn't seen Gigi in years. Why the hell would I kill my soon-to-be ex-wife for a woman I hadn't seen or heard from?'"

"Complaint reads that because you discovered her mother set up that abortion, not her that you decided to reunite with your long lost love. *And* you wanted to go find her," Gerard told him. "This investigation is nonsense and will go away, but I think the complaint might be from the woman who will inherit if Gigi doesn't fulfill her end of her mother's will. Here in the States, the press is talking up this story."

Sean picked up a glass of water and swallowed the cold liquid. He calmed his pulse, struggling to gather his thoughts.

"Who's set to inherit if Gigi doesn't meet the conditions of her mother's will? And what exactly are the conditions?"
"Mrs. Dumont's will reads desperate and pathetic." Gerard untied his tie. "I read it fifteen minutes ago. Gigi's to live in the house for a year, hold down a job, stay on budget, stay in the country unless her job necessities require a short-term change, and not get married or have a family within that year."

"For a full year?"

"That part of the will is unenforceable in any court. Any decent lawyer would tell her that."

"Gigi might not have asked a lawyer," Sean countered. "I think she may view this as penance and a way to free herself from her mother once and for all."

He added, "She's been grieving alone for a while now."

"Put her on the phone, and I'll tell her." "She's not here at the moment but you or I will tell her soon."

He paused then asked the question that had been on his mind since he'd received Liam's cryptic text. "On the day I married Jennifer, you talked about sex changing a woman. What did you mean?"

"Sean . . ." Gerard stopped moving and Sean met his gaze. "Are you having sex with Gigi again?"

No, but it was none of his brother's damn business. "Don't be crude." He'd soon have Gigi back and not be subject to family gossip. Sean set his jaw and refocused the conversation. "What did you mean at my wedding?"

"Look, Gigi should tell you. Lovers share secrets from their pasts, bro." Gerard crossed his arms. "Ask her about New York that summer, and tell her I still think of her as family. Liam and I worked hard to bring that bastard her mother hired to justice when you wouldn't listen to us."

Sean realized he'd missed something big. "What are you talking about? What happened? And no stalling."

He ran a hand through his hair, making the short strands stick up on end. "We tried to tell you, but you were adamant about moving on with your life." Gerard started pacing. "We thought it best to let you lead the life you chose. It's not like we had much of a choice. Accept that woman in our family or lose our brother."

"You're right. I am stubborn."

"We're all too damn stubborn in this clan."

Sean face tightened but kept his gaze alert. There was something Gerard wasn't telling him and he needed facts. Neither of them said anything for a few minutes.

"What happened?" Sean asked again. He kept his voice calm, but he refused to let this go. Gerard would speak. Then he'd get Gigi to tell him later.

"Her mother needed cash that summer. She intended to sell Gigi. I found out, and Liam and I called in a favor in New York. Some man had bought Gigi in New York. He found her and kidnapped her. We were able to send the cops to her rescue and she escaped unharmed. She wouldn't know any of that, other that her mother sent someone to attack her."

Sean's entire body shook inside, but he held together. "Lillian was something."

Gerard nodded. "Physically, nothing happened to her, and she never knew Liam or I helped her. Then you stood at that altar waiting, not knowing anything."

Sean sighed and closed his eyes. "Knowing Gigi was in danger would have stopped my wedding."

"Then I should have insisted." Gerard stayed quiet, and let Sean digest. On the day of his wedding, Gigi had gone through hell.

Gerard coughed then finished, "At the time, we hadn't known what to do. I'm sorry."

"I'm the idiot for not listening. Not that I wouldn't have married Jennifer shortly after that. Like you said, I was, still am, a stubborn man." Sean curled his hands into fists "You know that Jennifer married me for my money. She claimed to have no family of her own. I'd like to see if Jennifer was somehow connected to Lillian in any way other than neighbors. The timing makes no sense, and I'd guess Lillian and Jennifer plotted a few things together."

"If it were anyone else involved, I'd say you were crazy. But with Lillian, anything's possible. I'm on it." Gerard pushed a button on his tablet. "I'll let you know what I find."

Sean nodded then hung up the phone. He had so much to process and he wouldn't have a moment to himself anytime soon. That night he and Gigi would take the students on an evening cruise on the Seine. Tomorrow night, Gigi had the night off to see her friend Cary. In two days the big competition began, and he'd have the night off. But the answers couldn't wait until then.

Chapter 22

Gigi's feet hurt from walking up hill, and she longed to take a nice long bath in the huge tub in her hotel room, to forget tonight. A romantic evening cruise should be avoided. Besides the aches in her muscles would thank her for slowing down. She rubbed her feet and sighed. Tonight wasn't about Sean and Gigi. Tonight was about chaperoning.

Change was in the air, and she kept ending up on her own two feet. She wiggled her toes and relaxed her shoulders. She loved him and had stayed away to protect him. Maybe she'd been wrong.

Then she bit her bottom lip and stood up. She changed into her red dress and high heels. Red had a way of empowering her walk, and she needed the help. She kept her chin up in the mirror, and promised herself to follow through. Tonight she needed action or she'd pass out.

The red helped her get her head into her goal.

Sashaying off to the lobby, she enjoyed strange men appreciating her figure. That meant Sean would notice too. Her silver shoes clinked onto the marble, and she inhaled through her nose. She needed Sean to understand she controlled the situation. But the second she caught Sean's full attention and he stared at her up and down, every cell in her body activated.

"Ms. Dumont, you clean up good," David called out then Kendra clamped her hand on his mouth.

Sean's entire body tilted toward her and he gazed at her up and down again. Good. She said in a sweet voice, "Let's get going. Dinner and dancing sound amazing."

His blue eyes sparkled, and the fluttering in her stomach increased.

The students filed into the limo Sean must have ordered. He stared at her legs, and she took every step in a more dramatic way with him tuned in as her personal audience. The headiness made her want to jump and dance and run in the same millisecond.

Erica stopped her. "You made the transformation without changing your soul, Ms. Dumont, and you look pretty."

Gigi slowed down and gave her attention to her student. "Thanks. There is music and dancing tonight for the finalists. You'll have a great time."

Erica added, "I'm looking forward to meeting the French high school students."

"Good." Sean joined the conversation with his hand on Gigi's back, to escort them into the limo. Skin to skin sent her heart into a race, but she never once became dizzy. Her heart beat in her chest that echoed in her ears, but she kept her desire in check. She had a job to do.

Soon enough, the limo stopped at the dock, and she blinked. Lights from cameras flashed everywhere on the street. From a quick glance, her eyes burned and left her almost blind from the constant flash.

Gigi fought to see. Sean's hand squeezed her knee.

"Are they here for us?" one student asked.

"Who are these people?" asked another.

"Listen." Sean's voice remained firm. Her eyes locked on his. "Everyone walk fast, two at a time, and go directly onto the ship. The press cannot follow us onboard, but they are notorious for getting a rise out of you. No one say a word."

Kendra said, "But I want my picture in the news."

"You're not movie star Nicole Wyman." Gigi added fast.

Sean shook his head, "No, but you don't want this attention. They are not here to cover a school event," Sean warned her. Gigi bite her lip, and leaned closer to him to hear every syllable. "You want to be good famous, not part of a scandal you know nothing about."

"A scandal?" Gigi's mouth dropped to the floor. Had she done something? Or was this Collins family related. They were rich and targeted. She wet her lips, determined to defend him. "What?"

"I have news." Sean gave every one of them a stare down. Pressing her lips together, she became singularly focused on his words. "Back home, in Cape Cod, my brother told me someone complained I killed my ex-wife. It's untrue and false."

"Sounds like Mr. Murray," Raphael said. "He told my mother I earned a detention because I hit someone when it was really because he's racist. I'm the Hispanic boy at the school."

"Don't let them shock you and get an ugly picture." Sean turned to Gigi and took her hand. She kept her eyes on him, and studied him for any hurt. "I'll call everyone's parents when we get on board."

"You didn't kill her. It's the stupidest thing I've ever heard. You're the biggest pushover I know." Gigi's stared and witnessed his eyes snapped. She uncrossed her legs, and squeezed his hand. She'd never betray him. Sean Collins remained the sweetest most loving man in the world. She'd find whoever did this to him, and expose the truth. She told the students, "Okay, two at a time. Walk fast. Don't talk."

The boys paired up with girls. The students organized themselves three at a time, two girls per boy or two and two, and they ensured everyone had a partner. She kept a watchful gaze on everyone as they departed. She'd run out to save anyone one of them. No one would get to the students or Sean. Gigi pushed her shoulders back the moment she stepped out, and despite the shouts for a picture, she stood and waited for Sean to join her. She held her arms to her sides though she realized her red dress had a slew of cameras pointed at her. Her temperature skyrocketed, but she'd stand in anyone's way who even thought to hurt him.

The lights blinded her, but she refused to go anywhere until he stepped out. "Get out now, Sean Collins."

Behind her, he called out, "Gigi, I should leave."

"Too late. Face the fire and let's go." She stepped forward to give him room and soon he scooted out of the car. She inhaled the second his arm went around her waist. Then she smiled to everyone around them and led him out.

Once he started, he practically carried her to the yacht.

Reporters called out, "Is Gigi the reason for the murder?"

"Mr. Collins, anything you want to say to people?"

"Why does a billionaire who owns one tenth of the globe in various industries keep company with a high school teacher?"

Gigi stopped Sean, but kept her hands on his muscular chest and knew what she had to do. She stepped away and faced the crowd. "Sean is an amazingly wonderful man and father, and his family owns the companies . . ."

Sean kept his hand on her legs, then he picked her back up and carried her inside. Now she couldn't say anything else but his muscles warmed her. On board, he hugged her and whispered, "I asked you not to say anything."

She crossed her arms determined to argue with him if he dared let anyone push him around. Then she saw this battle plan left him winded. She tugged at his waist to keep him close and stared up at his stormy blue eyes. "I won't let anyone say bad things about you."

To prove her point, she kissed his cheek, then twirled away from him and the step. A smile formed on her face. She found her footing near the steps, then followed him away inside.

In the thirty seconds, Sean had gathered the students. She walked closer and heard him say, "You did amazing. Have fun and don't think about this for the next few hours. Ms. Dumont and I will be with the other chaperones downstairs."

Her group nodded and left the adults to join the teenagers. Every nerve ending in her body stood in attention. He pointed to the stairs that led downstairs in the yacht. "Let's go."

Gigi refused to let him go, took his hand, and joined the rest of the faculty downstairs. Her body must be flushing. In the glass she saw her flushed skin. She clenched her hands like that might help, but then two French headmistresses hurried over. "We had no idea you knew aristocrats, Ms. Dumont. This explains your intense knowledge of French."

"The Collins are Irish Catholics from Massachusetts. Irish boys are a dime a dozen there." Sean had not been blue-blooded aristocracy. He was her hero. The comment made no sense. "I lived in Paris on and off for the past ten years."

"Yes, but you speak too properly for where you lived," the snooty woman explained, then turned her nose up and beamed at Sean. "Monsieur, we take great pleasure in ensuring your stay is amazing."

Politics played a role in everything, including judging a language contest. The pretentious judge would never be good enough for Sean. Her skin tingled again.

Then he came closer to her. She straightened his tie then went in search of a drink. At the table, she picked up two glasses of champagne, and brought them back. Without thinking, she handed one to him. Then with his hand on her back, again, he whispered, "Thank you."

The two French women left, and she answered, "I've lived my life wanting you to be happy, Sean. Nothing's changed."

He traced his hand down her spine, and her body heated.

The Canadian group walked on last, and her mentor stared right at Gigi then asked, "What the hell happened, and who is Sean Collins?"

"I'm Sean." He waved.

"Figures, the American team." Therese, the French Canadian, greeted them warmly and finished, "Gigi, you have good taste in men. I thought you a snob turning men away when we went out for drinks. Had I known this man waited for you at home, I'd have understood. Next time, I will keep the men, or you can set me up with a date."

"Sean and I . . ." Gigi hadn't known what to say. Sean wasn't her boyfriend, or anything, was he? She gulped for air then blinked, straightened her shoulders, and shook it off. When her temperature returned to normal, she smiled uncomfortably. She must have looked foolish for not finishing her sentence.

Sean's grin never wavered and he answered, "Gigi and I grew up together. We lost touch for a while, but this won't happen again." Sean took her hand. "She's come home to stay."

"Sean, this is Therese." With Sean, her life improved dramatically, but she'd never once intended to stay in Hyannis.

Sean shook Terese's hand, and Gigi blinked as her heart beat wildly. No, Therese was nice, but she couldn't have Sean. She swallowed then finished, "She's been invaluable in helping me learn how the competition worked."

"Had I known I trained the direct competition, I'd have given less advice," Therese answered with a curious grin. "Now you must tell me. Are there more men like your Sean in your home?"

Sean said, "I have three single brothers and many cousins."

"Excellent." Therese kept her eyes on Gigi. "I still have options, then. Dear man, may I speak privately with my friend?"

Sean dropped his hand from her side, nodded, and left. Gigi's body turned cold the second his hand left her.

Therese directed them to the corner near the window and said, "You look confused."

"I am," Gigi said, heart thumping. Did she stay with Sean? How could she be good for him after everything? But then, he had no one else. "I don't know what to do."

"About the murder investigation? Do you believe—?"

"No." Gigi cut her off. "Sean wouldn't harm anyone. It's rekindling a relationship with him, stirring up my heart. Part of me wants to run for the hills."

"Are you mad?" Therese's face turned white and her mouth turned downward. "Is he bad? Treat you unkindly?"

"No, he's the best man in the world." Gigi would never allow anyone to speak badly of Sean. "I'm not the best woman. He deserves the fairy tale."

"Far too hard on yourself." Therese squeezed her arm. "Forgive yourself."

Loving Sean and being his wife were entirely different things. Her mother had told her to stay away from him for his sake, and she had. "I don't know."

"Then I hope he proves his worth in some way," Therese said. "And you must open up. One cannot fall in love if we don't allow ourselves."

"Why is it hard for people to understand? If you love someone more than anything else, you want them to be happy. That matters more than my personal desire."

"You only let go of people who don't want to be there. That man is standing over there, waiting for you."

Therese had made a point. Gigi's head stopped spinning and she listened. "Plato sold us on the idea for every man there is one woman who is his soul mate. Deny yourself love and you deny him his soul mate."

"My life is not philosophical." How does one argue soul mate? She shook her head. "Sean and I don't make sense."

Therese shrugged. "When does love make sense? Get back there and figure out your life with him. But, seriously, open yourself up. I will stay away because your my friend, but honey, not all girls are loyal when a man is that good looking and rich."

Gigi kept her head down, but followed her friend's gaze. Sean leaned against an edge of a wall, with his hands in his pocket, and spoke to some woman Gigi hadn't met. Gigi started toward him and instantly his blue eyes intensified at her approach.

When she reached him, he automatically touched her and his hand gently massaged her shoulder. "This is Gigi Dumont." She smiled at the woman and Sean finished, "Geegs, this is Sophie LaSalle. She's one of the final judges."

Sophie offered a small frown at Gigi then she smiled back. Gigi's mind swirled with Therese's warning.

Gigi hugged Sean and said, "In three days, the competition starts. The day before is full of practices."

Sean kissed her forehead. "Don't worry, Geegs. The students are ready."

The dinner bell rang, and interrupted all conversations. The students would eat above deck, while the chaperones ate below. The board in charge of the competition organized tonight for all the students to mingle with each other. But if anything happened, they'd be called by the ship's personnel immediately. Sean found a chair for her and held the seat for her.

Therese took the seat opposite, and ensured the judges sat away at another table. "I can tell you two definitely grew up together. For a new relationship, you act like people who've been married for fifty years."

Gigi smiled. "I was three, in the park, playing, when Sean found me in a tree then took me home to meet his mother."

Sean laughed, and her leg entwined with his under the table. "I knew what I wanted then and now."

"And your mother let you go to his house, at age three?" Terese's question hung in the air.

"No one says no to Sean Collins." He passed the bread rolls without missing a beat.

Damn. She'd loved Sean even then. Now she sat next to a man capable of so much. He'd make leaving again difficult. And the butterflies in her chest gave him more power than he realized.

The waiter brought out the salads. Knowing she despised them, she took Sean's tomatoes without asking and added a few pieces of her spinach to his plate.

After her first bite into his tomato, she caught Terese's upturned eyebrow. Gigi relaxed into the chair. But then a sudden rush of cold air hit her spine. She stood up and said, "I'm sorry. I have to go to the powder room."

Sean had no argument and she rushed from the table. At the door, she locked herself in, and stared at herself in the mirror, again. She never should have given Sean any room. Every touch sent warmness inside her and her face now had a permanent pinkness in it.

She closed her eyes and argued with herself. He should have the perfect wife and family. Her heart hammered on, and screamed for her to listen to the soul mate story. Her feet rocked and she held the vanity. She'd stopped believing fairy tales, yet her heart soared with hope.

Someone tried to open the door.

Her hands jittered as she reapplied her lipstick. What if the murder charges had surfaced to warn her away from Sean? Someone knocked on the bathroom door with more fervor.

Gigi cleaned herself up and opened the door. She nodded at the next woman and left to rejoin the table.

Sean stood at her arrival and asked, "Are you okay?"

"Of course. Tonight we'll talk." She rolled her shoulders and made the decision. Good. She surprised herself, but no other options remained on the table. "You deserve answers to your questions."

She stared at him over dinner. What exactly was she going to say to him? And since when were decisions this difficult?

Chapter 23

After hours of dancing with Sean, Gigi's feet ached, but her heart stayed fast and excited. His sandalwood smell lingered on her skin, and every touch of his skin on hers left her needy and lightheaded. She sat beside him on the way back.

The limo stopped and the group went into the hotel. She followed the teenagers and intended to supervise bed time. At the elevator, she glanced across the lobby, then froze. Antonio. Her hands curled up in her stomach and she cringed.

Tightening her shoulders, she gritted her teeth and formulated how to get that annoying gnat out of the way.

Sean's gaze followed hers, and he, too, stared at the dark-haired man.

She swallowed as Sean told the students, "Go to your rooms. Ms. Dumont and I will be up in ten minutes to check on you."

"No," she said. Sean should not be here. He had enough to worry about. "Sean, why don't you go upstairs and settle everyone in? I need to talk to Antonio. I'll be five minutes, no more."

"You don't have to be alone," Sean said as squeezed her hand. "I'm here."

"This is something I have to do." Antonio had details, knowledge. She'd face the man then go upstairs to Sean. "I'll be right back, Sean."

The elevator opened and the students went inside.

Sean refused to go, and instead, he threw his jacket on her shoulders then nodded at her. She wavered on her feet for that instant, but kept still until the elevator doors closed behind her.

Then her attention swung back to the bar. The lobby wasn't a good talking place. She pressed her lips together, gathered her courage, and strolled over to Antonio. "Shall we go across the street to the bar at the restaurant?"

Antonio bowed in agreement then grabbed her arm to escort her.

Gigi turned back and stared into Sean's face. She'd have had a different life if she had run to him.

At the bar, Antonio ordered a bottle of wine and two glasses.

As soon as the waiter left, she told him, "I'll get you your money. But I told you I needed the year."

"You get your picture taken with one of the richest men on the planet, shop at one of the most exclusive stores, and can't pay me my money?" Antonio asked, a dark scowl on his face.

"I didn't borrow or spend money." She crossed her arms. Her mother had set her up borrowing money with Gigi's signature on the contract.

Antonio represented just one of the unsavory people she now avoided. Gigi pushed her seat back. "I will pay you back every dime. You have my word."

The waiter brought them the wine and served two glasses. Antonio brushed his hands against her knees, then up her thighs. She squirmed, and he said, "You will get me my money tomorrow from your rich boyfriend. Otherwise our deal is off."

She shoved at his hands to get him to stop touching her. How dare he?

Then, *wham*! He flew off his chair and landed with a grunt on the hard floor.

Heart pounding, Gigi spun around in her seat and stared.

Sean leaned down and punched Antonio again.

The nearby patrons gasped, and Gigi felt her jaw drop open as she stared at the cheering teenagers behind Sean. Heat swept up her cheeks. She stood up and tugged on Sean's arm. "Sean, what are you doing?"

"We're going back to *my* hotel, where the staff will not allow this man back inside," Sean said calmly, though he kept his fighting stance toward Antonio. "Go, Gigi."

Her stomach clenched. She'd caused this. She had to fix this, especially
with the teenagers on the other side of the room watching. "Everyone's overreacted. Let's go to our rooms."

As she escorted the students away, Gigi craned her neck to watch the men at the bar.. Sean still hovered over Antonio and she could see that they were engaged in a heated argument. All because of her. Outside, she and the students safely crossed the street. "Wait in the lobby," she directed them. "I won't let anything happen. Be back in sixty seconds or less."

They followed her orders without question, and she walked back. The men continued to shout at each other, and she went next to Sean. She gulped and hoped to avoid escalation. Then she tapped his shoulder with her arm. "Please, Sean. He's not worth it."

Sean glared at Antonio. "Stay the hell away from her or you'll be answering to me."

"What do you plan to do? Kill me like you did that girl?" Antonio sneered.

Gigi stepped in front of Sean as he lunged for Antonio. "Sean, think of the students. They're waiting."

With a huff he stepped away, shot Antonio one last angry glare, then exited the restaurant.

They found the students in the lobby waiting, then escorted them all to their rooms for the night.

Gigi took a fast shower, looking forward to a good night's sleep.

With her towel wrapped around her head, she strolled out of the bathroom in another. She stopped mid-stride and clutched the towel to her body.

Sean sat on her bed.

"How did you get in?"

"I own the place, remember. Do you want me to leave?"

"No." She went to her bureau to grab clothes. She passed as Sean took her arm. Surprised, she tumbled and fell onto the bed, then accidentally knocked the towel off her head.

His warm flattened against hers.

She placed her palm against his chest. "Hold on."

"Why?" He kissed the nape of her neck.

Goosebumps formed on her body, and at the same time her nipples hardened. She covered her breasts with her arms, but her skin stayed electric and warm.

"We're supposed to talk," she said, though she could live without that plan. Seduction was a much better idea.

He stopped kissing her. "Good."

Drat. She kissed his neck, and hoped he'd go back to more sweet kisses and perhaps shed his clothes.

Instead, he stood up and handed her his suit jacket for a bathrobe. "We do need to talk. It's overdue."

"Yes." She dressed and crossed the room to sit at the fancy side seats designed for a noble person a few hundred years ago to have breakfast. The luxury did nothing for her nerves.

"Let's proceed in logical order. We were happy, planning junior prom." He followed her, and took the seat opposite her. "You and I had discovered sex too young. That's my fault, too. Tell me what the hell happened ten years ago?"

She couldn't meet his gaze. She stared at the vaulted ceiling. "You know . . ."

"Yes." He touched her hand, but she tugged it back. "You told me the night before you left, but you never blamed your mother. You claimed you did it on purpose."

"I lied."

"Why?"

"Your family is picture perfect. You know this about the Collins. Your mother and father are the fantasy parents." How would she ever make Sean understand? "My mother said I ruined her life the day I was born, and she'd not let me have a brat."

"You were practically adopted into my family, and we have money. You stayed at my house more often than your own," Sean said. "What happened? What did she do to you?"

"Mom decided she could not be a grandmother, not at that time." Gigi remembered her mother's face and why she had run.

Lillian appeared beautiful to others, but all Gigi saw was her hard, unforgiving face every time she had looked at Gigi. "Fun times."

"What? Nothing is fun." Sean's brow contorted as he tried to understand.

She'd told him how miserable her mother made her years ago. "I said that to cope." She gulped for air. "She needed money. My second stepfather had divorced her, taking his money with him. She didn't need me having a child."

Sean stared blankly at her. What had he thought? "You should have told me. You'd have never been alone."

"I couldn't face you or what happened to me. Sean, you were, are, perfect." She paused. "I ran away. I didn't know what else to do."

"Gigi, you never called." Sean shook his head. "You should have, and I'm far from perfect."

"You're my hero. You always were. I intended to, every night and every day." She laughed, a bitter taste in her mouth. "You deserved better, and I turned cold from fear."

"Of?" He stilled his face and never blinked. She pressed her lips together, unable to speak in that moment.

She turned her head away, not able to stare at Sean. It was easier to explain to the gleaming floors. She adjusted her hair, opened her mouth, stood up, then answered. "My mother's new husband believed me to be evil. He owned her, and I never wanted to see him again. They called me a murderer, blaming me for everything she went through. Richard McMillan said on the phone if I ever bothered my mother for anything, he'd put me away."

"What happened to Richard?"

She stared into Sean's eyes. Did he know this story? How?

She shrugged. "Five years ago he disappeared after he divorced her. I don't know, and I don't care."

Sean nodded, coughed, then stood up as well. "What happened to you in New York five years ago?"

"What are you talking about?" She gazed into his eyes and wondered what he could possibly know so much. "You were getting married."

"I made a mistake. And my brothers know. They say someone was arrested, and they helped you without telling you." Sean sat down. "What happened?"

Gigi dropped her arms to her sides. "Some jerk thought he had the right to touch me. Said Mom gave him permission. I said no and called the cops before moving back to Paris," Gigi explained in a cold voice. "And you up and married someone else that day."

Sean tugged on his ear. "You never picked up the phone. New York isn't that far from the Cape. had you done that, you'd have saved me from my marriage to Jennifer."

"I didn't think you'd even talk to me.

So what's the current problem?" Sean asked. "I need all the facts."

"Daisy Patterson. She owns Richard McMillan's—"

"Patterson?" Sean interrupted, and leaned closer to her. "This woman's last name is Patterson?"

"Yes. Why?" "Jennifer's last name was Patterson before. What does this Daisy have on you?" Sean asked.

She leaned back and crossed her arms.

Sean reminded her, "Part of letting someone love you is trust. I will help you."

Sean would help her. Gigi dropped her arms to her side. Sean's stormy gaze was not for her. "Daisy has tapes of me that could ruin my life now."

Sean shook his head. "What could be that bad?"

"Me believing I murdered our baby. I said stupid things. I was angry and sad and numb." She closed her eyes. "I called myself a murderer. At the time the video was taken, I believed every word. I was in a dark place and said stupid stuff. But now she intends to use it against me unless I pay her a million dollars. Once mother's will is finalized and I get her estate, I planned on paying her off with the money."

"We're not paying her off. And I don't care whatever is on the tape, and neither should you," Sean said firmly.

She stepped backward and shook her head. "I don't want to ruin my new life."

"It won't," Sean said in a straight tone. "I'm here now."

She bit her lip and stayed still. "I've been on my own."

"No, you never were. The police were near you in New York because my brothers sent them to you," Sean told her. "They know you were always my girl, Gigi. Collinses never give up, and you know this about me. It will have to be you that leaves me, Gigi. I'm not capable of leaving you and not wanting to help you."

"You're a glutton for punishment, Sean." Why were his brothers willing to help? "Thank your brothers for me."

"Your mother is dead now." Sean stood closer. "We lost years because you couldn't call me and tell me any of this?"

"Sit." She pointed. "We're not done."

He sat. She pushed a falling hair off her forehead, then decided to ignore her wet hair. "Antonio, the guy you punched . . ."

"Yes?" Sean asked with an intense stare. "He works for her. Says if I don't have the money in twenty-four hours then she's releasing the files, ruining my name, reputation, and everything forever. Now you have all the details." She shook her head. "Care to lend me a million dollars?"

"Geegs, I will fix this, then you will have no more excuses." Sean stood and went to the door.

She took a step toward him, but stopped herself. "Where are you going?"

"I'll be back. I have calls to make," Sean called out from the doorway before storming from the room.

She'd been on the run for most of her life. Now freedom meant she could return to Sean. Trusting Sean calmed her. She stared at the closed door, and her heart fluttered. Could he really help her? Did they stand a chance?

Chapter 24

Sean knew he needed to straighten this nonsense out. Ten years lost because of the crazy old lady who raised Gigi. He'd never call her a mother. Not to Gigi, not to anyone. The name didn't fit the woman who'd ruined Gigi for men, for life.

After leaving Gigi's room, he'd called Liam and Gerard, and they conference called in together. As they talked, Liam took notes on his computer. "Daisy Patterson. Jennifer Patterson. I'm not getting any hits right now, but let me dig deeper. McMillan owned a few businesses, and one of these must be linked to a Patterson."

Gerard added, "I'll look at the case file again. If Gigi doesn't get the money from her mother's will, there is a corporation named Rebecca Foundation, LLC, which, despite the name, is not a nonprofit. I'll take a closer look."

"Wait," Liam interjected. "I might have something soon. If I don't, when you get back home, have Mom fix up part of the house for Gigi to stay. Our house has more security than Fort Knox with the way the world is right now."

The rock in Sean's stomach churned at the idea. No one had threatened Gigi. To try and calm down, Sean took off his tie and button-down shirt then threw on a tee shirt. "Thanks. I wanted to straighten this out."

"No one is paying anyone money for a tape. If someone puts something illegal on the Internet or anything else that stupid, they'll leave a digital trace."

"Destroying Gigi's name is not what I intend," Sean said.

"Then look on the bright side. She'll be so grateful, she'll have to marry you when this is over," Gerard said with a smirk.

"Gigi deserves better. She needs to want to marry me, not feel obligated to." Sean gazed at the door. He needed to go back to Gigi. His brothers talked to each other on the video screen until Sean interrupted saying, "Good-night. I'll call back in the morning."

"Tell Gigi we love her and welcome her back into the family," Liam said.

With a heavy heart, Sean signed off. His brothers probably thought less of him. They'd dated countless women, and he had never let go of the one. Now he had to see Gigi. A few minutes later, he knocked on her door.

Finally Gigi opened her door, and quickly motioned him inside. She yawned. "I thought we were done. You charged off to be some white knight protector, saving me from my problems."

"They're being investigated as we speak." He stepped forward, and she stepped back. "You don't sound happy. What's wrong?"

"What's the payment for your help? What do you want from me?" she asked, sticking her chin in the air.

"What do I want?" His eyes widened. "Are you serious?"

"No one does anything for anyone without wanting something in exchange. It's what I learned out in the world." She raised a brow. "What is it you want from me?"

Did she not know? Or was she teasing him? "Gigi, I've wanted to marry you and love you since the day we met. Nothing's changed."

She kept her distance in the room, and circled to the other side. Her long legs exposed kept him glued to her shapely form. "Why haven't you taken over as the heir to the throne of your father's vast financial empire?"

Why was she being so difficult? Touching her would stop the trembling in his stomach. Kissing her would be a way to release of his fantasies today. "I don't want to talk about me right now. I need to know how you—"

"Fixing me is overplayed." Her shoulders went up and down and she stood near her dresser. She took a sip of water. "You are avoiding your destiny. You were the heir apparent."

He stepped closer to her then, keeping his voice low, he brought her into his arms. "I can't be the heir apparent. Not without you."

"That's not a good enough reason. Your family matters to you." He moved closer to her, and trapped her between the wall and him. Her mouth pushed up with her kissable lips close to his. "And you ignore when I say I need you in my life."

"Don't, Sean." She traced his chest with her. He settled her hands on his hips. "Don't, what? Tell me you love me, Gigi."

He intended to kiss her, but she turned her head away. Her eyes stared at a wall, and she refused to look at him. With his free hand on her chin, he gently turned her back to him. "Gigi, I need to hear it from you."

"And you need to be who you are supposed to be," she whispered up to him. He traced her body upward and kissed her lightly on her lips. "Running from who you are and want to be is stupid."

He held her close, and his awareness of her near-nakedness grew. Red-hot desire coursed through his body. "Damn. You don't shut up."

She drew him closer and kissed him hard on the mouth. Then she deepened the kiss. She pushed him backward onto her bed with her right with him.

He fell on top her. Her body trembled and his hand hovered over her moist center without touching her.

Gigi closed her eyes and let sensation overtake her. Sean pressed on the fold near her hips, and remembered how limber she had become when her muscles relaxed. "Hurry, lover. I can't stop, not now."

He kissed her again, and his fingers trailed to her stomach, massaging her muscles. He stared at her generous breasts, then took his time with her stomach. She moaned then she moved to her other breast.

"Sean . . ." Her breath caught in her throat and her arms tightened around him.

He took her nipple into his mouth and she moaned, arching backward. His mouth went back to the other breast. She continued to sigh and tremble. His fingers trailed south.

She played with his hair. "You're making me lightheaded."

"We both know you're hot for me," he growled. "I'm checking your temperature."

"Thermal at the moment." Her hands traced him, then she reached underneath his clothes, and squeezed his backside. He tore himself away then practically ripped off his pants. She traced her hands down his body. She needed him. Gigi had been the girl he'd loved and lost and found again. How did he get so lucky?

"Not a day went by without me wanting you back, Geegs."

Her skin flushed and she shivered. Then she answered him. "No… more… waiting."

Waiting tortured him, and she pushed him to join her. She was so close to her release. He kissed her lightly, rolled back, and found his condom. She winked at him, and he rushed. Finally, he positioned himself over her. They'd go slow later, much later.

She twisted her legs around him, drew him closer, and he trailed tender kisses on the nape of her neck. She opened for him and he thrust himself into her.

She let out a satisfied moan and her body set a frantic pace. One he was only too happy to keep up with, her cries sweeter than any symphony on stage.

Chapter 25

Someone tapped her on the shoulder. Gigi refused to move and jerked her arm under the cover. A strong hand traced her shoulder then Sean's voice told her, "You overslept, Geegs. The students must be hungry."

Fluttering open her eyes, she stared at her surroundings slowly, and tried in vain to filter out the light. Sean had opened the blinds leaving her no way to fall back into the blissful darkness.

Her eyes narrowed. Sean had totally dressed. She whiffed the air. And he was fresh from a shower smell. Then her lips opened. His body should be illegal for teenagers to see in a T-shirt and those jeans. She sat up, staring hard at his muscular torso, and remembered how complete Sean's size had made her cry out for him. With a smile, she blinked and asked in a yawn, "What time is it?"

"Eight forty-five. You have fifteen minutes, Geegs. The tour bus for Normandy will be waiting."

No. She raced out of bed to the shower. "I'll be ready in ten. Then we need to talk."

The towel he threw at her stopped her in her tracks. She stared at his blue eyes, and sighed. "Good morning."

"I like this greeting better." He kissed her forehead. "Morning, Gigi." He stepped back and told her, "Get moving."

She reached up and she caressed her throat. Then she ran. She closed the bathroom door behind her, turned on the water and hopped in the shower. Today she'd be an adult, and stick to her plan to run. The water refreshed her, and woke her up.

She had a slight reprieve from the lie she planned on telling today.

Running might not be her answer, but she couldn't let herself sway in this.

She tripped over her shoe in a rush, and still, she had no idea what she planned on wearing. She grabbed her robe and intended to take the first outfit in the closet. Then with a fast glance around the room, she saw a clean shirt and jeans folded neatly on the vanity. Sean must have taken care of her. Sweet. Sean was the best. She threw on her clothes, and exited the bathroom. He had already left the room. He must have gone downstairs. Then she found her shoes and a pair of earrings. She glanced around then left.

She tapped her shoes and waited for the elevator, which gave her a minute to think. In the daylight, the sun's rays argued with her intentions to fight with Sean and break his heart. She gulped. Tomorrow they had rehearsals and the day after the big competition. She folded her arms. Today was the day she'd end everything that happened with Sean. She closed her eyes and rocked on her feet.

The indicator light showed the elevator one floor above her. What would happen if she stayed? The clicked her heels one more time. She trusted Sean, but she didn't trust herself.

The bell dinged and she took the elevator downstairs to the lobby.

She scanned the area for Sean and saw him with the teenagers already on the bus. His blue eyes shone in that light blue T-shirt and blue jeans. She grabbed a cup of coffee from the buffet table, but she kept her gaze on him. How would she do this? He looked handsome and his killer smile made her knees weak, but she had to, for both their sakes.

Then his nose turned upward and he gazed down at her with a frown. Chest tight, she stopped. What had she done?

Chapter 26

Gigi had sat with her arms crossed next to Sean on the bus for the past hour without saying a word. He decided to call home and speak to his son. But his stare returned often to Gigi.

He hung up the phone and Gigi tapped her leg against him. Then she argued, "You never answered my question about your father."

"I'm not my father," Sean answered, but packed his bag up.

She whispered firmly, "Doesn't mean you are a school teacher or principal when your talent is in banking. Why are you here when you should be in a boardroom?"

"You wouldn't understand." He sighed. Gigi's no-nonsense edge meant she'd not let that go easy. Still, he'd always admired her tenacity.

She shook her head and crossed her arms. "Tell me."

Sean answered. "Dad inherited from his father, and my parents married, had the four of us, and lived happy ever after. I'm not the oldest or the youngest. I'm not the heir."

She shrugged her shoulders then stared at him in the eyes. "Bull. You are like your dad. You showed the most capabilities since birth, and your dad told you before your voice changed you were to take over the company," Gigi reminded him. "Does one of your brothers now want the job? Is that why you hesitate?"

"No," Sean told her. "I didn't want Jennifer to get anything else from me."

"Jennifer?" Gigi asked, offended. "She's dead now."

"Gigi, I worked for my father and planned on taking over again." He shoved a hand through his hair. "My ex-wife wanted more money every second of every day. When I realized what our marriage was, I cut myself off from anything she might want."

"Jennifer?" Gigi repeated. "She drove you to teaching?"

"Funny, huh?" He smiled, and his gentle touch coaxed her to relax her hands.

She dropped shoulder and sighed.

"Gigi, we fought over this daily. I don't want my father's fortune. This led to my job and, funny enough, you returning to my life."

She choked then patted her hand on his knee and shifted her body. "You are to take over. It's good. Your son deserves it."

"My son?" he asked.

She smiled. "Yes. Your son wants a father who's proud of what he does every day. If you are good at your job, responsible and loving, then you are everything they need to become capable, secure and responsible adults."

"My family is the most important thing to me, Geegs," Sean told her.

"Good. Your family is full of good people, and they need you."

"Let's talk about you." Sean's eyes lit up, and he stared at her full bottom lip.

"Me?" She gulped then blinked and dodged her gaze away from him. He remained still. Finally, she answered, "I'm hungry. I overslept and missed breakfast."

Something was going on. But he couldn't find out. The bus stopped at a brick building in the middle of nowhere. Then the bus driver opened the door and said, "World War Two museum and luncheon. Be back in two hours."

The students scattered to check out the museum, and he followed the group. Inside the memorial, everyone closed their hands around their body. The place had an eerie 'people have died here' vibe.

Gigi ran to stand next to him. He offered her his hand, but avoided her gaze and stared at the helmets, guns, and every other exhibit, and said, 'Cool,' 'Interesting,' 'Wow,' 'Intense,' and a variety of other one-word expressions.

He found history interesting, but his gaze often returned to Gigi, too. Something was bothering her and it wasn't the guns on the walls.

Every so often, she stroked his muscles and glanced around the room. Then she squeezed his hand in a pattern.

At the end of the tour, the students gathered close to them. They came to the room with the shoes and pictures that hung from the ceiling. The teenagers needed to be together to walk with the teachers through the Holocaust exhibit, effectively ending any one-on-one chance of a conversation.

Sean and Gigi took their time with the students, letting them form their own impressions and opinions.

The group stayed quiet and reflective for a short period. Tensions eased once they entered the area with the tranquil garden of hope, a stark difference to the horrors of the last room. Sean found that the natural beauty surrounding them enhanced how picture-perfect really Gigi was.

After they'd had time to debrief in the garden, Sean led the group upstairs to an amazing restaurant on the second floor of the brick building. At one point, the structure had been a factory and the design was more modern than most of France. The huge bay windows gave an amazing view of the surrounding countryside, and soon the mood turned chipper.

Sean and Gigi took a seat near the students but separate. The waiter brought the pre-selected meals to the table.

Sean took her hand. "Finally. What did you want to talk about earlier?"

The warmness of her hand and the happiness of the

students must have relaxed her. Her pupils were bigger. "I've lost my ability to fight."

"What?"

"I'm conflicted on what I want, Sean. You make everything come alive."

"Don't fight happiness."

"No. I'm not hungry anymore." She cleared her throat. "Sean, you and I are new and—"

"We're not a new item." Sean adjusted the hair that clung to her eyes and swept it behind her ear. "You're the woman I want to live happily ever after with."

"Sweet." She coughed. "But unwise. We hardly know each other anymore."

"What don't I know about you?" he asked as the server brought over the second course. "Is there another secret?"

"No, this isn't a secret."

He gave her space to finish her speech, but her soft gaze and kissable lips turned toward him gave him something to think about. He beamed at her, then pushed the plate in front of her, and handed her a fork.

"Eat, Gigi."

"If you think it makes me prettier." She took a bite of her food and smiled. "I've not been a happy person in a long time."

"You missed me. It's understandable. I often wondered what I did to you and where you were." "You moved on. Married another."

"You didn't save me, Geegs."

She rolled her eyes. "You joined the Marines. Was I to go to war and keep you safe there too?"

"No, but a letter telling me you missed me would have worked."

"Mom would have found out." She stared at her plate. "Tell me about Jennifer and what happened."

He glanced around the room, and most of the students sat at other table.

"Why?" he asked in between sips of his soup. "She's not a fun topic."

"Necessary though. Charges and photographers have popped into your life. Tell me about her." She took his hand for a few minutes and sat in silence. "I'm here to help."

"What do you want to know?" He pushed her spoon into her creamy soup getting her to eat.

"Tell me everything," she said. "How did you meet?"

"Nothing as memorable as you in your adorable pig tails." He took back his hand and she fed herself. "Jennifer appeared in town needing help with her car. I gave her a ride home, and at first she acted sweet, old fashioned, and intelligent." He shook his head. "I was blind. It wasn't until after we were married that I saw the differences."

"I'm happy it wasn't happy, but that's selfish of me."

"Why? I'd have killed that Prince Rudolpho or whatever his name was, or any man who hurt you."

"I'm saying things I shouldn't. You should be happy."

"You make me happy."

She shook her head and set her jaw. Then she cleared her throat. "Let's fast-forward. Where were you when she died?"

"At my parents' house surrounded by nurses, doctors, servants, and family. Cancer treatments were going well. This is why I don't understand the charges. She'd left me months before she died, leaving Patrick to me, with signed a full custody agreement. I was in the hospital, surrounded with well-caring people." He took another bite. "She walked the streets of Los Angeles wheeling her luggage without care. She never made it to her hotel, but I only know this because of the police call."

"You're right. The charges make no sense." She broke a roll, but kept her thoughts to herself. "I trusted you had nothing to do with anything nefarious. Why would anyone suspect now?"

He took half the uneaten roll on the plate without asking and answered, "No one knows. Gigi, being with you made the shock of the reporters easier."

Her face flushed and she darted her away then stare up at him. His warm gaze heated her, too. Despite the war going on in her head, he would win. She completed his life, and together, life would be better. All she needed again was guts.

"You're blushing, Geegs." His dimple appeared.

"The food is good here."

"Anything else?"

"Life with you makes me believe in fairy tales." She kept her gaze her eyes on her plate. "How's yours?"

"Life isn't a story with us, Geegs. You and I are alive." She kept her silence. He sucked in the side of his mouth, hoping he hadn't pushed too far. "It's good. Have some."

She shook her head *no*.

He picked up a piece of his chicken with his fork and brought it to her mouth.

She hesitated, pretended to be not hungry, but he didn't stop. His son played that delay tactic too. She slowly opened her mouth, and took the food he offered.

"Good, right?" he asked her.

"Food here is delicious. Thank you." Sean had a way of being a jerk. He had control issues and he never wrote a decent poem in his life. Yet with her in his life, he saw his partner who even everything else out. He loved her. And his heart told him she loved him back. She'd tell him soon. She squeaked out, "I like that we're friends.'

"Friends." Her word choice had him tug his ear.

But he refused to be detoured. He could play along for now. "Me, too. It's nice to have you on my side and in my heart."

"Heart," she repeated, and her mouth dropped open. He bite his tongue to stay silent. He wanted her to speak up on what was haunting her. Patience was his friend right now. But to wait sucked. His shoulders pushed back, and he stayed the course. He'd bide his time. She needed to open up. He loved her, so what stopped her?

With time, she'd tell him. He'd show her that she could. Gigi deserved the best possible version of himself.

Chapter 27

Sean decided something must be wrong with Gigi. She opened her mouth to say something for the third time and then stopped without a word. To help, he gave her room and left her alone on the bus the moment they'd arrived on the beach.

He kept a watchful gaze and she took herself up the trenches in rocks built by the Germans to shoot anyone who landed on the beach in an efficient, unyielding manner. Sean chose to head down to the beach and soak in the history on the shore. The students split up but knew the time and place they were to meet.

At the seaside, Sean threw a rock into the ocean and stared at the ripples. Had his grandfather experienced the horror show that ran through Sean's imagination at this memorial war beach or had it been worse? Gerard, his brother, and his grandfather talked more about the battle stuff, and Sean wished he had paid more attention. All four of them had served in the military, but Sean's life at that time had been a train wreck. The military had been a way to find order in the chaos.

With Gigi, life became normal again.

"Ahh."

Students screamed from above. His nostrils flared. Something had happened. He raced up the incline to get to them.

The second he joined them on the hill, Erica cried, "Ms. Dumont fell."

His heart nearly stopped. Then he raced to where Raphael and David leaned over, and shouted, "Take our hands. We'll pull you back up."

Gigi screamed, "Get back, boys."

Sean tapped them on the shoulders and slid into the dirt. "Hold my feet to leverage me when I pull her."

Every cell on his skin was alert and ready. He refused to let anything happen to her. He reached down, grabbed her wrist, and said, "Grab hold of me tight, Gigi."

She cried out, "I can't. I'm scared."

"I left you alone for ten minutes." His hand reached lower and circled her wrist. If he had to, he'd haul her up without her help. Then she reached up with her other hand, held firm to his arm and elbow, and gave him the leverage power to get her to safety. He tugged, and she came back to him without a struggle.

She started hyperventilating the moment he laid her on the ground beside him.

The students surrounded them and cheered.

She coughed. "Someone helped, pushing up on my leg. Check on the children."

Sean nodded for David to go count off and check on the others.

He straightened her clothes and checked to ensure her body hadn't been hurt. She appeared fine, and his pulse returned to normal. His heart beat again, and he kissed her forehead. "Who?"

"Someone in the trench below."

"We're checking on everyone." He lifted her head and had to resist the urge to kiss every part of her. She'd disapprove in front of the teenagers. His pulse had to settle on a hug, then he told her, "You're safe."

Her shallow breaths returned to healthy normal ones. Slowly, she told him, "Thank you."

"How did you fall off the cliff?"

Gigi sat up, and covered her face with her hand. "I stopped paying attention to where I was going."

"How the hell does that happen?" he asked in a huff. His heart raced as he wondered what would have happened if he hadn't arrived on time. He could have lost her.

"I was looking off in the distance and thought I saw ships. I wanted to see more clearly, and suddenly I fell. Someone below pushed up while you pulled. Hands were on my ankles, too. Who went down to the trenches?"

"We'll find out."

Gigi brushed her clothes and rocked to stand up. "Thank you. You saved me. Thank you," Gigi surprised him and kissed his cheek.

"I'd never let you go if you give me my chance." Sean's cheek heated.

She blinked and stared at him. Her lips opened to say something again. He stilled and waited, but she held her silence.

Kendra bounded up. "Is Ms. Dumont good?"

Without a word, Gigi spun away from Sean, and asked the girl, "Were you the one under my feet?"

"Yes. Are you okay? I freaked out when your foot dangled in front of me. I told Erica to hold me while I climbed up the trench."

Gigi hugged the girl. "Thank you." She then gazed at the rest of the teenagers. "You were brave together and smart. I owe every one of you."

"We all get 'As' then," David piped in.

Raphael added, "Mr. Collins did the most work, Miss. He knew how to get you."

Gigi stared at him and her soft tears struck him in the gut. How could she have put him through so much?

Chapter 28

After the beaches at Normandy, Gigi's body temperature calmed back down. Sean had arranged for the students to meet with local students for a mixer. Gigi loved the idea. Now her students had the opportunity to learn more about a local flavor of French and not her Parisian. Her ears had stopped the insistent pounding, and she relaxed. She quietly listened to her group interacting, and they asked quite a few questions.

The noise of the students dimmed the further into the garden they went. The French teenagers asked her students about Cape Cod and the movie sets there.

Kendra walked backward and whispered to Gigi, "Ms. Dumont, I thought the Europeans were smarter than us on geography."

"Of course. They get taught it more," Gigi whispered back to not offend the hosts. "They are smaller countries to our massive big country neighboring another massively huge country."

Sean added for measure, "Then why do they not know Massachusetts is not next to Virginia or Chicago? Our country is massive. They know country lines, but not state lines."

Sean had a point. But she explained, "Not everyone here tonight is on the path for college. Some are them are going to trade school. In the US, we give everyone the opportunity for college. You and your group are highly intelligent, making you see the world differently. We have plenty of people who live in our state who don't know where Virginia or Chicago is on the map."

Kendra shrugged. "I guess."

The girl wandered off, and Gigi decided to give the teenagers space to mingle.

She turned around and her shoulders suddenly became cold. Sean had disappeared somewhere. He had been there a second ago. Strange. She rubbed the back of her neck and wandered off. How many times today had she almost fallen into his arms, declared her love for him, and stopped feeding the black hole in her heart? Her heart raced near him, and she forgot about everything else. She fiddled with her necklace and discovered a path to a garden.

She fanned herself in the garden, but nothing stopped the heat. Despite the prickles on her skin, she followed a garden path in the evening moonlight and stepped into a well-maintained garden.

"No." Sean's voice wafted in the air from the right.

Gigi squinted and saw two people near what appeared to be an ancient ruin. Without thought, she trekked closer, and her mouth fell open. She stared and froze in place.

Sean had a woman with him, but she was on her knees crying.

Finally she crept closer. "What's going on?" Gigi asked, hearing the sharp edge to her tone. "Sean?"

"Gigi."

He stepped away from the woman, surprised, then came toward her.

She evaded his arm and asked, "What happened?"

"I received a text message." Sean showed her his phone with a message.

She refused to stare down at it, and she gazed straight at him.

"Don't look at me like I wounded you, Gigi."

"Mr. Collins is pulling his support of free trade against the general populace of French needs," the woman stated and she stood up.

"Politics?" Gigi took stock in the body language. The woman on her knees, Sean pulling away. Her brain yelled at her to not be stupid. Gigi swallowed. "No. Do not lie to me. I hate lies."

Scratch that she'd planned on telling one, but her lie would benefit Sean and hurt herself.

She stormed off, but Sean chased her. "Wait."

Every instinct was to run, but she turned to face him. With her hand on her hip, she asked, "What?"

"Gigi." He cleared his throat. "I don't know who she is. What you walked into was me saying no to the young woman wanting me or, should I say, my money. And there was a text."

He handed her his phone.

"You expect me to believe you would say no to her? She went down on her knees."

"I didn't do anything other than agree to listen to her 'proposal' which I thought concerned our schools and politics. Read the text."

She didn't need to read it. She believed him. Sean had this gullible issue every time he came near a woman in distress. He trusted everyone. Gigi pushed her chin in the air. "Doesn't matter, Sean."

"Yes it does."

"No. It doesn't matter. I believe you."

"Good," he said, and dropped his arms to his sides.

Gigi changed her mind and stared. She had spent years refusing to believe in happy-ever-after, and this nonsense needed to stop. Opening up meant forgiving the past. She'd have to try. If she found a way to prove it to herself, she'd tell him she loved him.

"I'm tired and my feet hurt," she told him. "Watch the children for a while. Don't go meeting another woman in there."

"Okay." He nodded then followed her direction and went back inside. "I've only ever had eyes for you."

Her gaze never left his, but she watched him walk away. She lost sight of him and her shoulders rolled. She let his comment sink in. Finally. He told her how many times now on this trip? She'd be a fool if she didn't listen. Clenching her fists together, Gigi swore she'd prove to herself and him that she was worthy. She loved him, and she'd find a way to show herself she deserved this love again.

She kept herself out of sight and out of reach for the next hour and snuck on the bus. Soon, she lost track of time and opened a book.

Her thoughts crystallized. Why that plan hadn't surfaced earlier she didn't know. She'd demonstrate to herself how love can win.

She nearly jumped out of her skin the second the doors opened, and she almost dropped her reader. Sean stood at the end of the staircase below, staring up at her.

Kiss him had been her first thought. Pushing her instincts aside, she asked, "What's going on?"

"We're going back to the hotel now. Students have a big day of rehearsals in the morning, and you and I will talk. Tonight."

Chapter 29

Finally, Gigi stepped off the bus and she immediately spotted Cary at the café across the street. She sucked in her breath and stared at the lights. Reporters had lined the street to get a picture of Sean on this trip, but at least they hadn't followed them to Normandy. And the door to the hotel was clear. A small blessing, if she had any say in what qualified. They entered, and she went over to Sean and whispered, "Cary's here. He's on the other side of the street with everyone else. I forgot he had some surprise for me. Take the children upstairs?"

"No. Go in. Then ask hotel security to go get him."

She nodded. He had a good plan. Then he waved for the students to go to the elevator. She trudged to the front desk and signaled for a clerk to bring Cary over to the hotel bar. At the lobby entrance, the bright lights of cameras still blinded her.

Sean motioned he had a call and she left and found a seat in a dark corner, away from the windows, and waited. Cary joined her a few minutes later, and she hugged him. "Hey."

"Hey, yourself. Did he kill his wife to be with you?" Cary took his seat ready to gossip. "I do love drama and that sounds better than any novella on air right now."

"No," she flatly stated. No one should suspect Sean of criminal anything. "He'd never hurt a woman."

"Good, though I do love a good obsession story. I was looking forward to helping him find new clothes, become friends, and all. I'd have forgiven him because he loved you."

Cary changed his tone from serious to excited. "I have my surprise for you."

Her friend had given her a place of safety for years. She trusted him, too, didn't she? "What is it?"

"I spoke to Mr. and Mrs. Collins—" Cary began.

She choked out, "What? Excuse me?"

"I spoke to your man Sean's parents. I know you, Gigi, and you told me before you couldn't be with the love of your life because his parents might object. I decided to straighten everything out for you. No one should give my sweetie a hard time."

Interference hadn't been necessary. "It's not his parents. You shouldn't get involved."

"Aren't you curious what they said?"

The tease in his voice made him sound happy. "What did they say?"

"If I can get you to go back to Sean Collins, and make up for lost time, then they'd cover the price of me owning my own theater, the wedding, and whatever else you wanted. Gigi, go back to Sean. You love him, and now I get money in this deal. We're going to follow my plan, and you need good clothes, not the drab school teacher garb. I made arrangements and the Kate Sparrow Company has already offered you a wardrobe for getting your picture taken in this time of need."

"Stop. I'm not pimping myself out for a few shoes and handbags."

"You need them, honey."

She laughed but refused to believe his nonsense. "The Collins are nice people. Good people, but in no way, shape, or form are you bamboozling them."

Sean took the empty seat at the table between Cary and her. "Gigi, who's bamboozling my parents?"

Cary smiled with his flirt face. "Sean Collins? You are

even more handsome in person. I thought the photos were doctored to make you look handsome."

Sean laughed, and she had no idea what to say. Cary had called his parents? Had Sean heard? She watched and waited until Sean shook Cary's hand. "Good to meet the man who took Geegs in when she ran away. I owe you my thanks."

"I didn't run away," she said. "I ran for my life. There is a difference."

Both men stopped talking and looked at her strangely. She maintained the silence and stared back at them.

Sean broke first. "Your mother makes the evil stepmother with a poison apple sound sympathetic." Sean stared straight at her. "When you left, we were seventeen. She forced you into doing something you regret. We were too young."

"Mom had the opportunity to earn a higher investment if she remarried," she said in a quiet voice. "I didn't want to put you or your family through my troubles, when mom sent me away. Your family deserves wholesome, and I was screwed up. I ran."

"Your mother spent more hours being jealous of you than parenting," Sean said. "Plus, she came on to me and every man in the family."

"She did?" Gigi blinked. "My mother had two distinct personalities. She flew into rages all my life, and I ran to you most of my girlhood to get away."

"Not when you needed me the most. But, Geegs, she can't hurt you anymore. She's dead." Sean fixed her hair. "You are no longer in danger."

Cary laughed to ease the tension. "I disagree. She's in danger if she doesn't follow her heart and marry you like she wants. Gigi gets jittery a lot. Is there any way you can marry her immediately, before you return home? Take off the pressure."

"No," Gigi shouted and stood up. "This is getting out of hand. I am not marrying Sean for you. You don't negotiate my life. I choose my life."

Sean and Cary stood up with her, and she stormed away from the table. She needed to figure out how to help Sean. She was tired of being the damn victim in her head to her mother's wrath. It was time to find a way to shut that woman up from her memory and prove to herself being happy with Sean would never be temporary.

Chapter 30

After Cary left, Gigi went to her room and washed her hair. Her dreams every night for years had been to return home to Sean. Now that she had opened her heart again, she realized how stupid she'd been. She needed proof everything changed. If she had that, if she found how to help him and that she made his life better, then she'd let go. She'd follow her heart.

She switched off the shower, changed into her night clothes, and left. Part of her was surprised Sean hadn't shown up in her room already. Her cotton T-shirt and pink leggings were designed for comfort and modesty in case a teenager needed her in the middle of the night. She changed into jeans and a nice blue top with a white undershirt, a pair of roman sandals, then she crossed the hall to knock on his door.

Sean opened immediately, but he stayed on the phone, and signaled he needed a few minutes. She nodded and understood. He had a business call. She bit her lip and listened. Could she help him with business? *Chief Financial Officer* buzzed in her ear. He'd be amazing at that job. Sean understood math, and glanced at the numbers on the desk and beamed her pride at him. He followed his dreams, and deserved everything. She took a seat at the window and reminded herself to look for her opportunity.

"Thanks. Looking forward to it, Dad," Sean said into his phone then he came up next to Gigi. He kissed her forehead and said into the phone, "Good-night."

Empowered, she stepped away, paced for a few steps, then her heart soared. She needed to find out what happened.

He hugged her from behind her back, then spun her around. "I did what you said."

"What did I say?" He finished his twirl and left her down back on her feet.

She focused. "What happened?"

"Dad suspected for years I'd end up working at Collins Holding and Trust LLC. I'd said 'no' in the past because I didn't want to give Jennifer any satisfaction. Then to have something to do, I pitched in to help, temporarily. Sounds stupid saying it out loud. The truth is working with my dad at his company saved my life, and you are looking at the official Chief Financial Officer."

"Yeah!" She hugged him. "You should have done that years ago."

He held her close, and she inhaled his wonderful body heat. Sean deserved the best. She took a second then a final whiff of him before she stepped back.

"I needed someone to push me," he admitted. "Now let's talk about you."

"Me?" What had she done? Her eyes opened in surprise. "What?"

"Your friend conspiring with my mother. It's okay. Mom still likes you."

She leaned closer to him, and she smiled. "Sean, what matters is finding that bridge—"

"What bridge?" He stared at her with his eyebrows raised. "What are you talking about now?"

"I'm trying to figure out how to believe in tomorrow." She held back substituting tomorrow for love. It wasn't right to get his hopes up.

"I want you. You want me." He traced her fingers. "This isn't hard, Gigi."

"Not yet." If she told him, she'd lose her argument. And she needed to be a good force in his life, and never turn into Lillian.

"Not yet?"

"Not yet," she repeated. She'd find her way of being worthy then say yes.

"What changed today? he asked in a subdued voice. "You can't believe I touched that woman."

"Never. I just needed alone time." She twirled on her heels. "I need to find my way to be happy, then to you, then we'll make sense."

"I don't understand," he told her plainly. "But you need to remember what's good. Just don't take forever, Geegs."

"Trust me. Just a little while. I'm trying, but first we need to help our students win."

"Do I have a choice?"

"I need you to trust me. Hopefully this won't take long." She held her breath and exited the room. Her heartbeat stayed loud but she heard the click of the door. She let out a sigh, leaned backward, and simply breathed. Sean deserved the best. She prayed she'd find a way. If she found a means to helping him, all would be right with her world.

Chapter 31

The students stared at her strangely. Gigi squared her shoulders and joined them for breakfast at the hotel.

Erica left her table and came over to Gigi. "Ms. Dumont, your pants are green and you're wearing your blue dress like a shirt."

She ran her hands through her hair. She had thought she had picked out the blue jeans and blue shirt. She gazed down, and noted how mismatched she was this morning.

Sean entered the restaurant, and she nodded at him with a stupid grin on her face. She stood up and told her students, "Stay with Mr. Collins. I'll go change, then we'll spend the day in rehearsal."

Gigi swirled to the door and bumped straight into Sean. He caught her and held her in his arms.

Feeling her cheeks heat, she said, "I put on the wrong clothes. Watch the students."

"Geegs . . ." He stared at her with his mouth open, but his shoulders slumped. "Okay. What is it you need to do?"

"I have to do this one last thing." She straightened and added, "Then you won't get rid of me."

Hope grew in her heart. She hugged him and watched his eyes grew larger. Without prompting, he nodded, stepped back, and watched her walk away.

Once in her room, she took off the dress and found her white shirt with a belt. She checked her shoes matched the outfit then left. In ten minutes, the bus would leave for their practice on stage without Sean. He had the day off while she coached.

In the elevator back down, Gigi forced herself to relax. Today she'd straighten out her life. Smoothing her pants, she stepped out of the elevator and approached Sean. "Morning."

"Morning. I ordered your breakfast." He continued beside her as she headed to the lobby. "Sean, everything will be fine today. Thank you." The twinkle in his eye fueled her hope she'd come back to him. She hadn't told him. A *but* appeared, but she shoved that annoying self doubt away. She would find a way to help him and convince herself.

"I still don't get it. While you are at rehearsals, I'm taking my jet to Geneva to have lunch with Daniel. With the charges all around, it's best to let the students have time to practice without me." Sean nodded. "If there are any issues, please call my phone, and I'll be back to help with dinner and nerves before tomorrow's big competition."

"Smart." She needed to think of her way of helping him. She'd prove to herself she had the right to be Mrs. Sean Collins. "Our students have an amazing opportunity. Today and tomorrow my life is theirs."

He had a strange glint in his eyes that caught her off guard. "You get your reprieve, but, Gigi, you're going to need to be fast with whatever it is."

Her spine straightened. "I agree. Sean, we both want the happy-ever-after."

He shook his head. Her hands inched up to her neck. The moment she found what she needed, she'd explain. She clutched Sean's ring. Then she sighed. Soon she'd run into his arms, tell him how she felt, and unlock a piece of eternal heaven in her heart.

Today had to go right.

Chapter 32

Sean de-boarded his plane and caught the limo to the chalet. His brother greeted him at the door with a bro hug. "Glad you're in the area. I've seen you more on this continent this year than our own."

"Holidays will force the hour drive from Boston back home where you belong, Daniel. Just buy a house," Sean said, and preferred to think about his family rather than Gigi.

"I'll probably move home in the next couple months. I'll know for certain in two days if I bought out Dr. Soliwitz's practice."

"Good." Sean's right arm twisted into an air fist, then he laughed. "If you do, Mom and Dad will double up forces on Gerard and Liam."

"Gerard owns a home in town, but stays on the North Shore a lot," Daniel said. "Some big case."

"True, but that excuse can't last forever."

"Gerard's good. Liam's the one they stress out about the most with his putting himself in danger." Daniel held up a glass, and motioned for Sean to join him. "You're the prodigal son, taking the glory, marrying your childhood sweetheart. You, Sean, are the luckiest one of us."

"I've not asked her. Don't jinx my pursuit. And you're the perfect one." He cleared his throat and admitted to his brother, "Gigi might not be forever in my life. She's acting skittish, and I need to tread carefully."

"What did you do?" Daniel's gaze narrowed on him, with his determined to fix everything attitude.

"I don't get it." Sean nodded. "Nothing. First she acted

happy, then her friend, Cary, spoke to our mother, and now she's on some secret plot. But she's less sad and completely focused."

"She hasn't said no?"

"No. And I haven't asked her anything."

"Smart man," Daniel said. "Don't throw in the towel on her yet. Remember what Dad always said when Mom went on one of her laundry or dishes rants after she never let us help her do anything. *She's nervous to be this happy. Ignore her for an hour.*"

"Gigi kept smiling a lot this morning." Sean's pulse calmed down. His mother had snapped out of her fits whenever her chores had ended. Sean took the advice. And for now, he'd focus on his plan and his brother. "You're the oldest and single. Doctors are the men that women on television talk about constantly. Doctor Steamy or Love or Hot. I want to hear about your women."

Daniel shook his head. "There is no one and to go out every night would drain me."

"Are you getting old?"

"No."

Sean smiled. "Good. Let's go play ball, keep you looking the part at least."

Daniel put the drink down. "It's on like Donkey Kong, baby bro. Remember who kicked whose butt the last time."

"Doesn't count. I had cancer. We both know I'm in better shape than you now." Sean laughed.

Both of them stood over six feet tall and had muscles from working out. He, however, played outside with Patrick and had more time to run than his always-working brother.

Daniel directed them to a basketball court, joking, "They called this the American men room."

"They have a professional team here." Sean took off his tie and button-down shirt. Exercise had to be better than sitting around waiting for Gigi.

Daniel bounced the ball over to him.

Sean grinned. He needed to kick his brother down a few pegs.

Chapter 33

Gigi tensed, unsure the second she stared at Sean. He stood at the entrance of the local restaurant near the hotel ready for dinner. The restaurant had a black bar separating the patrons from the street, and inside, the walls were a dark wood. The students' pressure to win was taking its toll on both her and the students, and tomorrow, their big day, weighed on everyone's spirits. The students had been nervous, jittery, and excited all at once. At dinner, the students chose to sit alone in the back again, and she tucked her shirt back in her pants. Then she went over and joined Sean at the door. "Hey. You coming in?"

"Hey back. How'd practice go?"

"Good. Are you going to watch tomorrow?" she asked, then escorted him to her table. He sat and then she offered him a bread roll the second she sat next to him.

"Of course. The press won't get in our way." In a booming voice for the students to hear, Sean said, "I'll be there to see my team, win or lose."

Kendra called back, "Mr. C, we're going to win. Bring your party shoes for tomorrow night."

The students laughed and went back to their conversation. Sean leaned closer. "Should I have scolded her for the nickname?"

"If they nickname you and say it to your face, they like you," Gigi whispered back. Her hand began to inch toward his. "It's better to smile."

"Are you ordering extra tomatoes for your salad, Geegs?"

"Thank you for letting things between us lie."

"'Lie' is interesting word. We'll talk about it soon."

Gigi gulped her water. She had no idea what to say. "Don't make me nervous when I have to be coach."

"Wouldn't dream of it, Gigi. I'm here for moral support."

Her entire body tightened up. She needed Sean near her or else she'd lose her nerve. She blinked and understood that wasn't enough. She needed to be strong, capable of loving him and standing up to him. The Collins family never backed down. She lost her ability to speak. Then she pleaded, "Is there anything I can do for you?"

He nodded. "Yeah. Help."

"How?"

"The woman I want back in my life is acting strange. What do you recommend?"

"Give her one more night. The pressure of the competition takes time from what she needs to do. When she has her moment…" Gigi stopped, realizing she was talking about herself in the third person. "I'll never leave you, ever."

His face beamed and he moved to get closer. "Good."

She nodded, but she had a tingling quiver throughout her body. She gulped, then she met his gaze. "I need to be free first. Give me this space."

He didn't blink but reached over to touch her hand. She sucked in her breath and hoped he didn't push. "Relax, Geegs. Your team has this in the bag. And I can wait."

Had she explained herself?

The waiter came with the meal.

You'll never be good enough for the Collins family.
Don't let sex get confused with love.
I don't know how I ended up stuck with you.

Her mother's ghost hit her stomach, and left her tied in knots. If she didn't justify to herself her mother had been wrong about her, then she shouldn't be with anyone.

"Gigi, eat. You're white as a ghost. What's wrong?"

"I'm fine." She gulped.

"No, something serious is wrong with you. No one is going to attack you. You are right here with me."

"Wait. I forgot." *Attack.* She had forgotten about the threats. She'd been focused on Sean. "I don't have the money to pay off people. If the video goes viral, I'll lose my job and what's left of my reputation. I have a right to worry."

"I have it under control. You won't lose your job. Focus on the students." He squeezed her hand.

Sucking in her breath, she blinked. He should be focused on the murder charges.

Wasn't this supposed to be the other way around? She'd targeted helping him first, and forgotten about the dangers. "How do you know?"

"I own the school."

"Not about the job. How will you find the blackmailer?"

He shrugged. "I made arrangements to corner whoever this is and find them."

She trusted him. He'd take care of her.

He continued with his hand on her knee. "Once this is done, we can focus on our lives."

Her pulse ached for him to hold her, but she dared not. Not yet. "Thanks. Let's go to bed, then tomorrow face the big day."

Tomorrow she had the competition. But her heart beat faster. Maybe she'd find her answer, too. Her shoulders lightened. Soon, she'd find her way.

Despite everything, she found herself starting to believe in happy-ever-afters again. But first, she needed to find her place in this one.

Chapter 34

Sean kept his phone on 'silent' but he kept the mobile in his hands for most of the morning. At ten o'clock, his brother Liam called. Sean took note that his students were not yet on stage and proceeded out into the lobby. In a corner, he leaned against the wall and tried to appear casual and happy. "What's going on?"

"You're not going to be happy, but I'm handling it."

Not good. "What?"

"The video was put online. A few hundred people have seen it, but my IT guys have isolated the computer that uploaded the video. I'll be there in three minutes, and most of my men have blocked the world from viewing. I'll call you back in ten minutes or less."

Sean kept the painted smile on his face. Gigi's video had the potential of going viral. When the video was deleted, her blackmailers would be caught, and no one would care. Who in Hyannis would dare question her if he stuck to her side? He inhaled deeply, pocketed his phone, and retook his seat in the theater.

Ten minutes on the clock dragged as he stared at the time above the stage. Gigi had stayed backstairs, and he'd never had the chance to tell her any developments. Unease plagued him as he shifted in his seat, then crossed his legs. The program read that the students were not performing yet.

This was taking too long. Sean quickly returned to the same spot he left. He decided to call his other brother, the lawyer, Gerard.

Gerard answered on the first ring. "Hey, I planned on calling you any minute now. I have news on Gigi's mother's will."

"Beat you to the punch then." Good. Sean checked one thing off his list. "Who owns the Rebecca Foundation and inherits if Gigi doesn't?"

"Jennifer, your dead wife," Gerard said. "Which means the money reverts to you because she died before the divorce proceedings. Even if Gigi gets disinherited, you give it all back to her. She won't lose anything." Gerard changed tone. "But, Sean, this gives you motive for those charges. I'm waiting on a callback from my friend at the station who needed my help a few years ago when a prostitution scandal almost destroyed his family. I'll get who filed the complaint this morning."

"It wasn't Gigi." Planting his legs a little apart signaled Sean had been ready to pounce, but what could he say?

"I know. Two minutes."

Sean told Gerard, "Thanks. Call me the minute you hear anything. I want everything cleared up."

"Sure. Talk soon, bro."

Sean stared at the digital clock on his phone. Besides having more money than he'd ever be able to spend, his brothers' career choices had useful perks. Liam's experience meant he picked out the men on his special team, but Sean paid for everything.

Once, the British and the Brohmin's of Boston had kept the Irish poor in the past, but the Collins family had a proud heritage to keep up. Their money was a spit in the eye of the past. The marble statue of his great-grandfather in Boston, Patrick, the poor, penniless Irish boy who'd become mayor meant no Collins would ever go backward into extreme poverty. Sean would keep up his end of his family heritage.

The wait made his stomach turn so Sean walked away and peeked inside the theater. His students were not on stage yet. Good. He returned to his spot against the wall and finally

Liam called him back. "It's offline. The files have been deleted. There were a few downloads across the country, but we'll have those places searched within the hour. The normal online viewer is getting the message now to delete the video because it contains viruses. This is much smaller in number than another case, and we have more money for this operation."

"It's good it's under control," Sean said. "Who put the video online?"

"Right now we know it was a woman, short blond hair, blue eyes. We have a picture and video surveillance, and we're running it through the databases for an identity match."

"Daisy is real then." Sean closed his lips and nodded his head, pretending not to be surprised. There were too many coincidences and links to Jennifer. Whatever the women had planned, they would fail. "Gerard said Jennifer owned the Rebecca Foundation."

"I have to go. I'll call you back." Liam hung up.

Again not enough answered, and Sean hated waiting. He went to the bathroom, splashed water on his face, and returned to his seat. His students had not made their appearance yet, but Gigi sat in the front row now. With her hair tied back in a bun, she epitomized the naughty teacher fantasy. He blinked and told himself later. He found his seat and calmed down. The students must be on soon.

A cool short-haired blond woman took the seat next to him. He ignored her at first, but she made quiet scratching noises for attention. The same way a cat begged for food. He rose his eyebrows, then asked, "Ma'am?"

"You're Sean Collins, no?"

The fake Georgia accent stuck out. He knew people from the south, and her voice mimicked a bad joke.

"You're the one who owns a school and is engaged to be married to the porn star while still up on murder charges."

"Excuse me. Gigi is nothing of the sort." He clamped his hands down on her arm. "Are you Daisy Patterson?"

"Who?"

She sounded defiant and proud. He glanced at Gigi in the front row. She had no idea, and he'd keep it that way. With his free hand, he redialed his brother, and let him listen in to the conversation. "Daisy, what made you think you could frame me then show up here?"

"What made you think you could turn my sister into a gold digger then dump her?"

"Your sister?"

She struggled to take her hand back, but he held firm.

The curtain opened and the students came out to have an entire conversation in French.

Sean glanced to check to see if someone answered the phone. Confident, he said loudly, "Daisy, Jennifer was your sister? She never mentioned you."

"Did you ask her about family or did the marriage get based entirely on what she gave between her legs, providing you with your heir?"

"My son is the best thing that came from Jennifer." People stared at them.

Then sirens blasted outside the theater.

Gigi's gaze met his across the darkened theater. The question and protective lioness stare she threw his way made him pause. To appease her, he nodded at her, but Sean let the woman go. Then Daisy took off running. Gigi's gaze never left his until he nodded at her then ran after Daisy.

The sirens disrupted the performance.

Then Sean heard the woman's yell. Then his brother Liam surprised him and met him in the hallway. Sean didn't ask, but took a step toward the clacking of a woman's heels in a rush.

Liam stopped him and explained, "She's caught. I wanted to tell you I was in the area, but I didn't want to tip you off. Daisy's been taken away and is en route to the FBI for transfer back to the states."

"Can you silence the noise and let the children finish?" Sean asked. Gigi needed to be told.

Liam gazed at Sean, then stepped back. "I'll go outside."

Sean stared at his brother who went to speak to the French authorities. Sean waited for the police cars to leave, then returned to his seat.

Gigi's gaze met stepped back into the theater. She smiled at him then returned her attention to the stage.

He gave her a curt nod to indicate he handled everything, not that she'd understand anything.

Two hours later, the announcer said, "First place goes to the new American team from Gloucester, Massachusetts."

A warm feeling swept through Sean. They had won. And he only hoped that with Daisy gone, he'd win back Gigi, too.

Chapter 35

Gigi's mouth fell open as she shot out of her chair at the reception dinner. She rubbed her eyes and stared. Liam Collins had joined Sean in the back of the lobby. She'd talk to Sean later about love. Liam and the sirens could not be a good combination. Liam worked for the CIA. She muttered under her breath and had a few questions. "What's the big adventurer doing here? Shouldn't he be off on some mission to save the country from terrorists?"

The woman next to her asked, "Who are you talking to, Miss?"

Gigi went closer to the men. What if there had been news? She kept her feet together, and refused to let them shake. Both men mingled with people on the other end of the room and every cell in her body stayed on alert.

Her legs twitched. She pasted on a smile and adopted an excited strut meant she'd appear normal.

The French Prime Minister's ambassador to the United Nations was sent to the student international assembly. Everyone gathered the crowd around him for a speech.

Gigi held her glass for the toast afterward and focused on the speech about the youth being the future and international communication the keys to success for every person on every continent. Gigi half paid attention though she saw on the students' faces that they were enthralled.

She inched closer to Sean and his brother but lost sight of them in the crowd.

Drat. Then every part of her body grew goose bumps. Sean had that affect on her when close.

Suddenly, Sean's hand took her arm, and her heart raced. She turned into him. She leaned in to kiss or hug him, but her arm ached from his determined grip. She struggled, and he let go. Then he directed her out into the hall outside the lobby as the bureaucrat spoke. She stayed on his arm, but fear gripped her throat.

He guided her behind a statute and whispered, "Geegs, the video went viral for about ten minutes today. Every copy and download has been contained."

"Are you joking?" Her body chilled. No. Wait. Sean had he saved her. She lost track of everything else for a minute.

"Sweetheart, I wish I was. Now the good news."

There was the good news. Was he being sarcastic? She crossed her arms. People had seen the video. "What was on it?" She refused to stare at Sean. She stared at the statute and fidgeted with her necklace. "What can be good?"

"The FBI has Daisy in custody. She put it online and was caught. She cannot inherit from your mother if you don't, and I have the power to ensure you get the money no matter what."

"How?"

"She's Jennifer's sister."

"How is your ex involved?"

She hadn't understood.

He took a step closer. "She owned Rebecca Foundation, which means if you lose, I just give everything right back to you."

Her eyes opened wider. "I need to talk to her."

"Why?" Sean stared at her strangely. "Let's let this go now."

"She tried to destroy me. I need to talk to her. Find out why. Can you get me there?" she pleaded. "Why would anyone seek to humiliate me or help my mother who's in her grave?"

"I know why. My ex-wife was her sister. Didn't you hear me? You shouldn't talk to her."

"That isn't enough. What else do you know?" Sean had to understand her. "How does Jennifer or her sister that relate to me or my mother?"

Sean's gaze became clouded, then he clenched his hands together. "Your mother left Jennifer the remainder if you never collected. She also received money from her. Turns out your mother was Jennifer's step mother for a year before you were born."

"You married my step-sister?" Gigi asked, and scratched her head.

"She never told me of her family." He sucked in his breath. "You have no one to pay off anymore. Everything is done. If anyone who saw the video ever says anything bad, I'll deal with it."

"Why?" Sean was protecting her. She remembered the boy, but the man in front of her remained her strong hero. "Why would you do that? I never did anything to prove I loved you back."

"Prove?" His eyes gazed at her, confused. "I love you, Gigi. You deserve to be happy, and you next to me is all I need to understand you love me."

"No. It's not enough. But first, I still want to talk to her." She'd face this woman then thank Sean and his family. "I had a whole plan on how we might end up together. It's gone now. And I need to see her. Then we'll talk about us, about the future."

"Why?"

"My mother screwed up my life. I don't know why she hated me," Gigi said. "I never will, but I want to talk to this woman. I need a clue on why my mother hated me."

"I'll talk to Liam."

She sucked the air around her and gazed up at him. Now she had to find a way to help Sean.

Chapter 36

Sean escorted the students to the post competition goodbye festivities on his own. Gigi stood nearby, but remained silent.

The students hopped on the bus, and Sean followed them. She waved the group off.

Then once she saw the bus leave, Gigi strolled from the hotel down Avenue Gabriel to find the embassy. Clenching her fists, Gigi hoped her feet would carry her toward Lillian and to confront her now.

Sean had loved her. She still loved him. A silly grin formed on her face at his face in her memory. Lillian had gone too far. To prove to herself she could be happy again, she'd tell off this Daisy. Collinses have the strength and gumption to survive anything.

At the street corner, she waited for the light to turn. Whenever she slowed down, her hands fell to her sides.

Soon, she was at the embassy.

The three-foot metal barricades formed a long line to get into the embassy. She folded her arms and waited in line with people filing for passports and visas for her appointment.

Someone pushed behind her. She had forgotten Parisians did not stand in lines well, and she had to fight the crowd that would push her down and walk over her. An hour later, she filed close enough and the guard near the ten-foot black fence took her name. He checked his list then told her, "When you enter, you are to go to the right and tell the guard outside the door your name, Miss Dumont."

She nodded, but her skin prickled at being singled out. The guard stared at her until she said, "Okay, thanks. Go right."

He pointed with his hand to the gate and she stepped forward. Then he buzzed her in. She tugged at her ears and walked away from the crowd. A lot of stares followed her, and her steps forward became even more awkward.

She squared her shoulders anyhow. She had come here for resolution and to see this Daisy in person. What would she say to her though? How did she confront someone who tried to sabotage her adult life with her past depression for profit on the Internet. Someone who'd helped her sister hone in on *her* Sean? "Hello" sounded too polite.

Gigi hesitated at the door. She had nothing to say. She'd come to look the woman in the eyes.

Gigi crossed her fingers, took a deep breath, stepped inside, and told the guard her name.

The guard nodded. "Mr. Collins' guest. Wait here."

She nodded then reminded herself *get mad*. She clenched her fists and punched the air. She had been publicly humiliated. She should imagine one of those major slaps to the face of the woman who'd done this. Gigi hid her arm behind her back. Not that she could. The police or whoever was in charge would stop her, though in her mind she visualized the scene. Good. Now she needed to figure out what to say.

The guard signaled for her to go into the next room. Gigi straightened her clothes, and desperately tried to figure out what she'd say. The doors in front of her made an electrical noise signaling to open. She pushed on the door. Inside, Liam waited with a woman sitting in a chair. Upon closer inspection, Gigi breathed easier as she gazed at the woman's hands and feet chained to the foot.

"Gigi, this is Daisy," Liam stated in a directorial tone, then closed in closer to her.

She froze, and Liam squeezed her hand in support. Sean's little brother had grown up into a gentleman.

"You okay?"

She nodded at Liam, and he told her, "You have ten minutes."

She stared at Liam and waited until he left the room. Then she gazed at the woman, Daisy. Gigi bit her lip and squared her shoulders. She needed to yell at her and tell her off.

Gigi opened her mouth but nothing came out.

Daisy's eyebrows rose and she shook her head. "Age hasn't helped you, sweetie. Lillian always said you were an ugly beast."

Daisy had short blond hair and a petite frame, with the basic demeanor of a pretty girl who always got whatever she wanted. Gigi hated her type. Her mother had had the same appearance. Gigi opened her mouth to scream, but instead, she squeaked, "Hey."

"Not the brightest bulb in the pack, I see."

No words formed in her throat. Daisy sounded like her mother. Without intention, Gigi flinched. To calm down, Gigi rubbed her neck and tried to sound firm. "Did . . . Lillian . . . ?"

Daisy interrupted with a sneer. "Did Lillian think you an idiot undeserving in her will? Yes, Giovanna, she did."

Damn. Gigi blinked rapidly and attempted to sound in control, "I was threatened with character destruction. I'd have lost my job. Why did . . . ?" She took a breath, needing to stop the tremors in her voice. She swallowed, then she finished her question in one breath. "Why did you put it online?"

"Are you scared? Lillian thought you slow, but from what I can see you have no voice, no guts."

A squeak escaped her mouth. What? How had she let her win? Turning on her heels, Gigi knocked at the door, which opened immediately.

Liam helped her out with his hand on her back. "I called Sean. Take the car outside to join him."

"But . . ." Gigi lost her voice. This wasn't supposed to happen. She'd intended to be the victor, and vanquish Lillian from her head. She'd then run to Sean's waiting arms. Clenching her jaw, she couldn't see that being possible now. "We made plans."

"You shouldn't be alone," Liam told her. "Don't listen to trash, Geegs. Go home. Marry my brother and stay away from bad people."

Cackling from behind her wafted in the air, and Gigi rushed out the door. Today had not gone according to plan.

The car waited outside for her. Without an argument, she stepped inside the vehicle. Nothing had gone as planned, but she hadn't known what else to do. At lease Sean wasn't here.

The car drove toward the students' celebration. Her heart sped up as she pictured Sean's warm face. She needed to hold him.

Today, her past had stolen her energy to fight.

Chapter 37

Sean had the students in a circle talking to each other. Sean stared at the half-opened door as he listened to Erica say, "Every one of my dreams came true here."

Then Gigi entered the room. She took his breath away. The students stopped talking and giggled at him. The same thing had happened to him in high school, every morning. She had walked into class to sit next to him and all he ever saw was her.

Now he clenched then unclenched his fists three times, reminding himself to focus. Everything in the room became clearer and Sean saw Gigi's eyes watered. His gut dropped into his stomach because she was near tears. "Students, go inside and dance with the others. Ms. Dumont and I need to talk."

Gigi nodded at him, covered her face and stepped back outside.

Raphael told Erica as they left, "If one of the French boys tries to kiss you again, it's because you left my side. Stay close."

Erica shook her head. "I handled it."

At least the boys understood they needed to protect the girls. Sean knew his responsibility, too, and proceeded outside to the gardens. He caught up to her in a few long strides and stopped her with his hand on her shoulder.

Instantly, she turned into him and buried her face against him.

Rocking her softly, he told her, "Gigi, it's okay. You're safe, now."

"I couldn't speak to her," she sobbed. He continued to hold her. "I wanted to prove I was strong, but I'm not."

"Doesn't matter. The case is solid."

"You shouldn't be here. I don't deserve you. I lost," she said while she hugged him tight. "Losing means I get to live with regrets for the rest of my life."

"No, it means you're out of practice. I'm not going anywhere." He hugged her then kept her in his arms. "You don't need to win anything. You ran away and lost the ability to fight back, sweetheart. Going there today, alone, was a big step forward for you."

"Stop being nice to me." She pushed on his chest to get away, but she pushed half-heartedly then gave up. Instead, she chose to stay right there, in his arms. And her tears ran into his shirt. "I shouldn't have come here."

"Yes, you should. You need more work. Tonight we'll work on you getting angry," he told her but she never left his arms. "You don't have issues getting mad at me."

"You changed…"

"How? I'm still the guy who loves you."

"Not what I mean. You took responsibility and grew up nicely. I need to be like you," she said. "I swore I'd find a way to prove I was good enough for you."

He cocked his eyebrow. "Seriously, is that what's been bothering you? Gigi, you do help me all the time."

She stared up at him, looking wide-eyed and confused. "How? You're always protecting me."

"You pushed me to talk to my dad," he whispered. "And you listen to me."

He kept his voice low but clear. "Go to the hotel. The students want to leave the party soon, go get dinner on our own, and take pictures near the Champs Elysee. We've passed it a few times, but they want to stroll."

"I'll go." She gulped for air. "Thank you, Sean."

Watching Gigi sashay away, hope struck him. Had she not seen how she'd changed his life? If she needed proof, he'd show her tonight.

Chapter 38

Gigi hadn't wanted to cry, but the second she closed her door in the hotel, the dam burst. Crying earlier on Sean's shirt had been the only the surface. She stared hard at herself in the mirror, and she was so sick of the sad face that stared back at her.

No. Her entire body shook. Gigi clenched her fists on the vanity. She refused to cry.

But the question kept pounding in her head. Why had it been acceptable to her mother for this Daisy stepsister to post something on the internet about her almost attack? And why hadn't Gigi been able to say anything? She clutched her pillow and collapsed on the bed. Then she realized her frustration came from not having the words. And her unresolved mother issues had stopped her from trusting Sean.

Gigi sat up and went to the desk. She'd make a list of life with Sean and her hopes and dreams versus a life alone without him. She rummaged through her bag for her tablet and furiously typed out her thoughts. She expressed the questions and what she needed to say out loud.

Three pages later she hit the save button.

On page after page, she kept saying how she had to tell Sean she loved him. If she told him, she hoped this darkness would shrink in her heart. She went to the bathroom and decided to take a long bath in the huge tub then wash her face.

Tonight she'd beg Sean to forgive her for being an idiot.

Sean had been there for her today and whenever she needed him.

The tub eased some of her nerves, but Gigi dressed. And the group wasn't back at the hotel yet.

Unable to sit, she decided to venture out. Time alone wasn't her friend. Sean and the teenagers would be gone for hours. So she picked up the phone, "Cary, I need to go out."

"Shopping?" he asked in a high-pitched voice.

"Yeah, okay." She nodded. She had seen a gorgeous pair at the department store the other day and wanted a second opinion. Shoes always made her more confident, and she had saved her money all year to pay off a blackmailer. Now that the blackmailer had disappeared, she could afford a slight splurge. "Sounds good. Meet me."

Good. No tears with Cary allowed and she let out a sated sigh. She'd meet Sean for dinner, and new shoes would help her be a new Gigi Dumont.

The driver from the hotel took her back to the store without question, and she went inside.

The salesclerk from the other day greeted her. "Gigi Dumont?"

"Yes."

"I hoped you'd return. Mr. Collins' promise sounded amazing. Let's get you ready for him," the sales clerk offered in rapid French.

Gigi stepped back. "I'll be making a smaller purchase today. I don't have Mr. Collins' credit card, and there is no tip from him."

"Clothes help improve our mood, either way." The sales clerk blinked, but guided her inside. "Let's find you something amazing to show off your figure."

"I saw a pair of shoes to start with," Gigi said.

The salesclerk directed her to the department where her eyes focused on the Vivienne Westwood heel reminiscent of nineteen forties elegance meets softer colors of this century. The tiny details made a major statement. Pointing to the shoes, she waited to try them on.

Nodding, the salesclerk departed and Gigi took a seat. Seconds later, Cary arrived. "Shopping and not second hand. I like Sean Collins' style."

"You like his deep pockets," she told her friend.

Cary snarked right back, "And you like what's inside his pants."

She threw her head back and laughed. "You are crazy."

"Gigi, I told you to talk to him and get everything out there, but you skipped a few steps. I will convince you marrying him and fighting with him is much more enjoyable than life on your own."

"Stop," she said. "I am not discussing Sean with you."

"Cause you love him and are confused. Sexy men can have that effect on us," Cary said. "Where are you wearing these shoes then?"

"Tonight for dinner . . . with Sean."

The salesclerk returned without the shoes. "Please come with me, Ms. Dumont. Everything is ready for you."

Confused, Gigi and Cary followed to the backroom where there were seats and champagne

The salesclerk directed them to sit.

"But I wanted to see the shoes," Gigi protested.

"*Certainmont*," the clerk said. "But first enjoy the private viewing. I picked a few items that would look amazing on you."

"I cannot afford . . ." Gigi said, but Cary propelled her into the seats.

"I've never been rich. Indulge me. I want champagne." Cary smiled and inspected the bottle. "It's a good year."

Giving up, Gigi took a seat. Models walked out with a few nice outfits in-between the more crazy. She admitted to appreciating a dress and two separate more levelheaded outfits. She sipped her wine, and Cary laughed. She raised her eyebrows at him. He was on, like, his third, and she needed to get going. "I'd like to try the shoes on now," Gigi told the salesclerk. "The salesclerk finally presented the shoes. Gigi tried them on and admired them in the mirror. Nodding, she said, "It's time to pay for the shoes only. Thank you for today."

"You enjoyed the three outfits, too?" the sales clerk asked, quirking her eyebrow and smiling.

Shrugging, Gigi answered, "Yes, they were very pretty, but I am buying only the shoes."

"I understand completely, *Mademoiselle*. Give me a few minutes." The sales clerk's word bubbled with eagerness and she bounced out the room. "Finish your champagne while I take care of everything."

"Great." Gigi sat down next to Cary. "Today was fun. Thank you."

A few minutes later, the clerk returned, handed her a card and a receipt, but she squeezed her hand a little too hard. Gigi tugged her hand back as the clerk told her, "I sent your packages downstairs to your car. It was a pleasure to help you today."

"Packages?"

The clerk held her hand on her hip, "Your man is waiting for you, *non*?"

The salesclerk left in a hurry while Cary escorted her away. Gigi shrugged and decided to let her doubts go. She pocketed the receipt and went downstairs. Cary said goodbye to her at the front door with an outrageous hug. "Can I drop you off somewhere?"

"I have a date close by. Handsome man, not as good as yours, but sexy. Get home to get ready for your man. Sean loves you and you love him. Don't throw it away," Cary said. "Now, goodbye, girly."

She hugged him then hopped into the car. Her shoe purchase sat on the seat beside her. She let her head rest on the seat and she closed her eyes.

The car arrived at the hotel, and she got out. Photographers snapped pictures at her, and Gigi rushed to get inside.

"Wait, Mademoiselle." The driver stood at the open trunk, revealing multiple packages.

She ran over to him. "What are those?"

"Your purchases, Mademoiselle. I'll send them to your room."

Gigi rubbed her chin. She'd been set up and she'd walked right into it. The woman must have billed Sean for everything there. She ripped open her bag, and read the receipt. The three outfits and every accessory were listed. No wonder the woman had taken her measurements after the first glass. Today had been a set-up. Sean had likely promised her a huge tip if she'd sold Gigi clothes, but Sean hadn't been with her today.

Gigi paced then another photographer snapped her picture. She rushed inside and went to her room. When Sean came back, she'd explain the purchases and send them back to the shop.

Everything could be returned.

Chapter 39

Gigi dropped her clothes in a heap on the bed and decided to try on the red dress in her room.

She had to send it back, but she finished with the zipper. Then she stared at herself in the mirror. She looked better than she imagined in the A-line. Movie stars wore dresses that flattered in this fashion. Now she understood. She snapped a picture of herself in the mirror for the memory then tugged the zipper to take it off.

But the zipper stuck.

She tried harder, but the zipper refused to move. Wiggling hadn't helped. Then the phone rang. She told herself to breathe and picked up the phone. "Hey."

"Gigi, we're downstairs. Students are hungry. Hurry up."

"You were supposed to call me before you left," she said. She stared at herself in the mirror. She needed to get the dress off.

"There wasn't time. Let's go."

Sean's voice sounded apologetic. She held the phone for a minute. "Okay. Be right there."

Inhaling, she stared at the price tag. One more time, she reached around her back with her arms and tugged on the zipper. No luck. The dress refused her commands.

She dropped her hands to the side and stared at the door. She'd set up a payment plan and give him this money back if she wore this out.

She gulped. The phone rang again. She saw it was the front desk and hurried out to the elevator.

She stepped into the lobby a minute later and heard Sean Say, "Wow."

Sean and the students dropped their jaws, and she stopped in her tracks. Heat rose in her body. "Is everything okay?"

"You look beautiful," Sean said. His gaze confirmed his approval.

Erica motioned with her fingers to turn around.

Gigi smiled at her and took Sean's offered hand. He smelled of cedar wood and manliness. Smiling, she told everyone, "Let's go get dinner."

Sean held open the door for her. Her stomach fluttered up to give her a jolt in her heart. The students walked ahead of them, and she told him in a quiet voice, "I told the salesclerk I came for shoes. She put this on your credit card through a trick after she solicited my opinion on clothes. She charged your card, and I'll figure out how to pay you back."

"I offered her a substantial reward to do that, if you remember. It's more my fault than yours." Sean fixed his belt, not meeting her gaze. "And I approved the charges when she called me."

She stopped and dropped his hand. "You what?"

"She called. I approved the order, and she earned her tip."

"Well, I don't know what to say," Gigi said.

"How about thank you."

"Okay, thank you." She smiled at him, and he escorted her from the building.

The white façade and streetlights gave Paris an ethereal brightness. Yes, tourists often complained the city had dirt and a certain smell in the air, but Gigi always found the place far more magical than anything else. Paris and the French language gave her safety and allowed her to rest.

At the hotel Meurice, in the heart of the city, Sean and the boys waited for the girls and Gigi to go inside. The girls all held their breaths and smiled before Gigi joined them. Staring ahead, she saw the glamour that stopped them cold. A wall of mirrors, a white chandelier, white chairs made for royals of previous years, the restaurant was old world glamour.

So, this is why the boys wore suit jackets. As few curious people stared at them, Gigi kept her head up, and followed behind Sean. Then the waiter brought them to two tables.

Listening, she waited for Sean to finish ordering for her. She enjoyed chicken capers, broccoli, but no. He ordered her mussel soup. Gross. Her face wrinkled. Then he ordered for himself onion soup. She pressed her lips together, and kept her mouth closed until after the waiter left. "Why did you order that for me?"

"Don't scowl. Why didn't you tell me you don't like mussels, Gigi?"

"You know I hate the slimy things." He had done this on purpose?

"See. You lost your backbone. How do you plan on living your life for yourself if you cannot remind me you hate the soup?"

"Hey, that's not fair." Gigi pouted, not wanting to hear him. "You knew I didn't like it."

"Enjoy the soup," he said. "And tonight you are meeting me in the gym before bed. You still need to work on this."

She bit her tongue. Not loving him remained impossible. "We have to be up early tomorrow for our flight home."

"I know the schedule. Don't fight me on this one. You know I'll get you there either way."

She tilted her head up. Sean had always been gentle and easy to lead. Perhaps his marriage had made him harder, and she'd forgotten that he could be stubborn and determined to all others.

She sighed. Okay. The gym sounded innocent enough, and Sean had a plan. She kept her mouth closed.

Soon, the waiter brought out her choices, after all.

The second dinner ended, Sean directed the group to the street. "Make sure everyone has a buddy, then you have one hour to window shop. Meet us back at the Arch D'Triumphe. If you need anything, call. And stick together."

"You said that," Raphael answered back.

Gigi called out, "Don't be smart."

Sean wrapped his arms around Gigi. "Go."

The group rushed down the street, excited for their moment.

Sean hugged her. "Is there anything you want here?"

She imagined Sean's kiss. His face stayed behind her, yet so close. Her pulse raced and knees weakened. She turned into him and leaned closer to his hard mouth and firm body. Her entire body warmed. She gulped and her face flushed. "Grand Palais is still one of my favorite museums, even if the students voted it off the must see list."

He offered his arm, and she turned back around to the street. He was everything, but she held back and hesitated.

His earthy laugh warmed her heart and they walked into the glass ceiling building. She twirled around and stared. They had the place to themselves. She stepped away from him and gazed up at the night sky. She laughed and twirled again. "When I first moved here, this place remained under construction for years. When it reopened, I kept imagining myself a princess who could see the world without touching it. I spent hours here, reading in that corner."

She pointed to a corner.

Without words, Sean followed her directions. "Here?"

"To the right a little more."

Sliding down a few places, he asked, "You sat here?"

"Yes." She sat next to him, but he repositioned her into his lap. She laughed, and then his hands went to her face, directing her lips toward his mouth. She sighed and kissed him.

They were alone.

Fire, wind, tornadoes, earthquakes had less of an impact on her than his mouth on hers. Every part of her dug into his warmth. Her hands raked his body, and he let out a deep, guttural sound of approval.

She moaned his name in response.

Whatever else happened, this kiss made her toes curl.

Chapter 40

An hour and five minutes later, Gigi and Sean met up with the teenagers who waited patiently, seated on a bench. At the last second Gigi saw a smudge of her lipstick on his white collar. She rubbed his neck with her hand, and brushed out the soft fabric. He stared at her, confused. She gulped and needed to ensure no one saw evidence of what happened. She smiled at him, continuing to rub. "Good to go."

"Am I presentable?" he asked, winking at her.

"Yeah, you're perfect."

Sean stepped away and gathered everyone. "Let's return to the hotel. Tomorrow we have to be up early."

A few students grumbled, but they strolled back toward the hotel after snapping maybe twenty more pictures. Sean shepherded them, and she followed. He had the group moving, then he held out his hand for her at the hotel lobby. "Let's get back. When we get back, change into sweats and meet me downstairs in five minutes."

"I don't know . . ." She took his hand and lost her thought.

He must have sensed her confusion. "There are a few things we need to face. We're going to the gym for your workout with the punching bag."

Every time she gazed into his eyes or stood next to him, she wanted to curl into him.

"You're staring at me with a blank expression."

The doorman opened the hotel for them, and the students rushed to the elevators. Sean kept his hand on her back to escort her inside. Soon, she figured out how to open her mouth to speak. "Sean, you and I are . . ."

She lost the word. *Fit?* No, her life made sense with him. Match? No, everyday of her life, she thought of him. The words never materialized in her throat for what to say.

The elevator dinged, and the group went to their floor. Sean whispered into her ear on the elevator, "You run scared, afraid to admit a lot of things."

She bit her tongue. Yes, she remained afraid.

"You didn't always. You used to speak to me."

Everyone ran to their room without much coaxing. Sean and Gigi remained in the hallway to ensure everyone made it back safe. Soon, they were alone in the hallway with no movement for a few moments, and she said, "I couldn't manage to get the zipper down on this dress earlier. I might not be able to go to the gym."

"Not an excuse." He spun his finger. "Turn around."

She picked up her hair and turned to give him her back. His hands on her back warmed her, but she trusted he'd be a gentleman. The zipper stuck in the same spot near her bra where it had earlier. However, he muscled the zipper and the fabric loosened.

Then his fingers traced her exposed back, and she leaned backward with his hands on her body. Sean kissed the nape of her neck then told her, "Change, Gigi. We're going to the gym."

Sighing she went to her room. Slipping the dress off the second the door closed, she delicately packed the expensive piece in her suitcase. She hadn't wanted to snag anything about the lovely designer piece.

Then she found her sweatpants. She had packed them to run in the hotel emergencies. She never packed a fancy sports bra, and settled on a beat up T-shirt meant for bed. She stared at herself and shrugged. It was the best gym outfit she had.

Then she tied her sneakers on and raced downstairs. Whatever Sean planned to do in the gym sounded safe enough. If he wanted to work out with her there, she'd be fine.

She walked into the hotel gym a few minutes later. Sean waited and continued with one last push up. He wore gym shorts that showed off his toned muscle legs, and a wife beater. His strong muscles captured her eyes. The door hit her backside, and she had half a mind to turn around and leave. She must appear a hot mess compared to him.

She glanced around. At least no one else worked out anywhere. She cleared her throat, and Sean turned around holding mitts out for her. "You expect me to box?"

"No. Put these on, Geegs."

She inspected his hands, and noticed his scars. He's done this without gloves. She asked him, "Why are we here?"

He tied the straps tight on the gloves, and reminded her, "I need you to get angry and punch the bag."

"You are being stupid," she argued. "I'm not violent."

She folded her arms together, but he unfolded them and finished tightening the gloves on her hands. "Arguing with me is a good step for you, but you need more aggression. My family is Irish and we'll flay you alive, Gigi. Did I ever tell you your mother ran her hands down my brothers and me, offering herself?"

"No."

She stood there frozen, unable to move. Sean pointed her palm and put one of the gloves on the bag, indicating she should hit it. "With me, I told your mom, hell no, fast. She told me I loved with the wrong girl, and that you never cared about me."

Unable to budge still, Sean picked up her other gloved hand and guided her punch. "With Gerard, she became far more aggressive. She took her shirt off, and threatened to call people in the room and say he started it. Gerard's callousness grew leaps and bounds after that."

Her mouth formed an 'o' then she asked in a quiet voice, "How did Gerard get out of it?"

"Gerard told her he didn't care what she said because no one in their right mind would ever believe he'd touch an old woman like her when he had a buffet of models downstairs wanting him."

Gigi stifled an inappropriate giggle. "Gerard still appears to have his attractive jerk quality too him. Why does he fascinate girls?"

"Hey, now," Sean said. "We're talking about your mother. You know, the woman, who videotaped you over indulging in alcohol and depressed?"

She shook her head. "Don't, Sean."

He hit the bag himself. "Don't what? Remind you that your mother strapped you down to a table with a doctor, stood over you, and ensured you had an abortion weeks after you received your driver's license?"

Shocked at the unforgiving reminder, Gigi remained quiet.

"You ran away from her to a different country, leaving everything you ever knew behind. You passively want to forget the past and forgive her now because she's dead."

Gigi covered her ears with her gloved hands. "Stop."

"I'm not doing anything to you," he said. "Hit the bag and think it's her."

"I don't want to scream and shout. That gets no one anywhere!" she screamed at him.

"Gigi, you're already yelling. Now go to the bag and hit it."

"Why?" She stomped her foot. "Why is this important to you?"

"Pretend it's Lillian, your dear old mom. Tell her you're not taking her crap anymore." Sean pointed.

Gigi walked over to the bag and hit it once. "Good, now I'm done with this."

"You hardly hit it. Pretend the bag is your mother." He crossed his arms. "That woman deserves far more than one gentle tap."

In her head, the bag transformed into her mother's cruel, laughing face telling her how ugly she'd turn out to be and how no one, not even Sean, would want her because she was destined to be fat and ugly. She closed her eyes and the bag stopped talking. She faced Sean. "Don't make me do this."

"Gigi, you need to let it out and scream," Sean said in an even voice. "Until you scream and shout, you'll never move past it. I promise one day I'll be an accidental jerk because I've had a bad day, and you're going to have to tell me to shut up. I listen when told."

She stared at the bag again then rushed at it to throw a punch. Then two punches, then three. "Is this what you want from me?"

"Tell your mother to rot in hell," Sean said from behind the bag.

"This is stupid," Gigi mumbled to herself but she tightened up her body and shouted, "You were my mother. You were supposed to love and protect me like every other mother on the planet. But all you ever did was insult and hurt me when I wanted you to love me. Whatever I did to you wasn't equal to what you did to me, Mom."

Gigi had no idea how many times she hit the bag. She stopped and wiped the sweat off her brow. Tears mixed in, then she shouted more. "I never wanted to be like you. Why did Dad die when I was a girl and not you? You deserved to die before him."

She crumpled to the floor. She had no more punches to throw.

Sean sat next to her, rubbing her back and holding her. She regained some energy, and Sean pushed a water bottle under her nose. Her nose honed in on his almond-scented soap. How? She turned into him, away from the bottle.

He patted her hair. "Your mom can never hurt you again, Gigi. She's gone."

"She sent the Daisy woman to go after me and sent Jennifer to you."

"You're not to blame for my screw up with women." He sighed. She continued to hug him. He fixed her hair. "We'll figure out what's best for us, but know this, Geegs, I will protect you."

She trusted him. "My plan was to find a way to prove myself worthy of you."

His arms around her were exactly where she'd want him to be. She knew they were an impossible pair, and she had no rights to him. He reminded her, "Sweetheart, you push me in the right directions."

She reached up to his neck and stood on her tip toes.

His kiss created stirrings inside her.

She'd never quenched this thirst, and she needed more. And his lips tasted better than anything else.

Chapter 41

Gigi refused to end her kiss with Sean. He stepped back slightly, and she stepped forward. Explosions of love lit up her heart. She wanted to tell him she loved him, but he deserved a woman who had the ability to speak.

She licked her lips.

"You confuse me. You do know this?" he asked her with her shirt halfway up her chest. She smiled in his arms, and wiggled to get him to lift off her shirt. "This was my solution."

"I appreciate it," she said, and her hands trailed to his gym shorts. She rubbed his backside and smiled. He hadn't worn underwear.

He rolled away from her on the floor mat. "Geegs, there can't be a future unless you speak up."

"I'll be more assertive." She frowned. Sean thought too much right now. She refused to think. "Lock the door."

"Not what I meant."

"I'm saying what I want right now." She inched closer and kissed him. Hesitating for a moment, he gave in, and his hands circled her, crushing her into his muscles. She won and hugged him tight. His lips on her skin made her body ache with need.

Hot she moaned and his hands caressed her breasts.

She arched back for him. She'd never have enough of him.

His tongue darted under her bra, and her breasts turned into aching pebbles from his licks.

A moan escaped her lips while her head fell back. Damn.

He repeated his actions to the other, and she helped him lose the remains of her bra.

Unable to think, she tugged with his hair and wiggled.

His hands played with the elastic band of her sweats. Gigi wanted to kick off her clothes and rip his off. She traced his shirt upward on his muscled torso, needing to feast her eyes on him.

Sean grunted and threw his shirt.

Then he went over to the door. She sat up and covered herself, but then he returned.

"No one is in the hall." He offered his hands to help her stand, and she followed. Bending her neck with his thumb, he kissed her aching flesh. "We should go upstairs."

"Wait." She needed him now. Cooling off for any sort of minute meant a chance to breathe. She needed to not think things through. She tugged on his hips, and arched him closer. "Now."

He laughed and held her close. Then he kissed her.

She walked backward.

She sighed, and needed him to hold onto her forever. Trusting Sean, she licked the inside of his mouth, teasing him. Her backside pushed up against elevated padding. Helping her sit, he took her sweatpants off her.

Finished, he stared at her nakedness. And she wasn't shy. Not with Sean. She stared up at him.

Sean had filled every night's dream and passing thought. She needed him inside her. Her hand circled his manhood, playing. She kissed the nape of his neck.

"Geegs." He gasped out her name, sending a ripple of excitement through her.

Her mouth trailed down to his shoulder and her hands massaged his muscles. Slowly, she teased his erect penis closer to her waiting vagina.

With his arms on her, she reclined back onto the bed or

whatever tannish thing she lay back on. Then she opened her legs, allowing him access to her center.

His hand traced her body, and she directed his manhood to her core. He took her hint and plunged into her.

Her body quivered and ached for more every time he moved. She lost her ability to think and focus.

He moved, and she huffed out a frustrated breath, needing him back inside her. Moaning her satisfaction, he entered her body over and over.

She lost herself at some point. And he moved deeper inside her.

Somehow she heard his whisper. He kissed her ear and said, "I love you."

That was all it took to send her over the edge.

Her mind came back to her at some point, and she surveyed her surroundings. Sean had found a massage table, and she had enjoyed every minute. He sat next to her after covering her with her own shirt. She sat up, partly dressed, then held her hand on his back. His arm covered his face. "What's wrong?"

"My intentions were honorable when I demanded we come to the gym."

"I see that. I seduced you," she admitted. Loving someone shouldn't be this complicated.

He laughed, and his earthy rakishness had a certain charm to it. "Gigi, when we get home, you and I have unfinished business. I'm not letting you get away from me."

"I seduced you. Don't blame yourself," she argued, not listening to whatever doubts her mind could imagine. "Paris is the city for lovers."

He kissed her forehead. "It's the City of Lights, Geegs. Get dressed. We have to get you upstairs with no one seeing."

Her body glowed from the day. Once again, he'd protected her, and she listened to him. While she was slipping her sweat pants back on, Sean fixed himself in his shorts.

She watched his muscular butt and she blushed. Today something inside her had changed. She stuffed her panties into her pocket while she asked him, "Where's your shirt?"

"I'm a guy. I threw it in my bag. Let's go."

He escorted her to her room and held the door open for her. Did she kiss him? Awkwardly, she stood there, then he brought her into him for a kiss. His arms around her waist, she tasted him again, and her body shivered in anticipation. She'd never have enough of him.

Sean hugged her and her body had trouble calming down. He whispered into her ear, "I will have plans for us back home."

"You do?" she asked, confused. "What plans?"

"You need to start believing in happy-ever-after, Geegs." He winked at her. "I'll convince you."

He dropped his arms to his sides, took a step backward, and then walked away. She watched him, unsure what to do.

She closed the door behind her and sank into her room. Wasn't she supposed to prove herself to him? She had lost her handle on this situation, because right now she wanted to run to him and scream she loved him more than life itself.

Chapter 42

Gigi sat on a plane, unsure what had happened. Now they went home, back to Cape Cod, with the victory completed. Hours into the flight, the teenagers remained excited.

Sean spoke on his phone about business and politics every time she came over to him. And she hadn't known what to say to him, but the quiet unsettled her.

She'd earned his love. Somehow. Now she needed to stay safe.

The best part of the week she'd never forget remained Sean holding her close again.

Gigi kept her head down, and hoped to avoid all attention on the ride home. Her face would have a permanent blush with her thoughts. So she held a book in front of her but never read.

Erica bounced to the back of plane. "Ms. Dumont, are you tired?"

"Yeah, the past twenty-four hours have been taxing." Erica whispered, "Mr. Collins took a new job on this trip. Do you know who will be our new principal?"

Sean never should have to settle for anything. She shook her head no. "I don't know if he's made a choice, honey. I'll ask him."

"No worries. I'm happy to be going home." Erica bounced back to her seat with the rest of the students, but Gigi's mind swirled on the question. Had Sean made any decisions? What home did she ever have? He'd been busy making plans for his life, and she hadn't found a way to prove herself.

What could she do? He had a full life. A son. A full-time job. And a generous, protective heart.

He hadn't needed anything.

Gigi stared at Sean who stood with his pilots. She overheard something about clearance.

Then he smiled at her. She motioned for him to sit near her. He nodded and took her up on the offer. But he kept his phone on his leg. "Did you need to see me?"

"Have you made any decisions?" she gulped out.

"Quite a few. Which ones are you questioning?"

With fists clenched, she asked, "Work. Do I have a job, Sean?"

"If you want it, sure. I'd never hurt you. That's up to you. Did you doubt that?"

He pushed a piece of her hair back in place, and she hesitated. "No. It was a lead-in question."

He traced his hand down off her face, then squeezed her knee. "Speak then. What do you want?"

"If you are taking over the CFO position for your father, who will be principal?"

"Do you want that job?" His eyes read surprise. "I didn't think you wanted it."

Speak, she reminded herself. Furiously, she answered back, "No, I don't. I'm a teacher, and unsure of my future. I'd be a terrible principal. I wanted to see if I could help though."

He smiled at her. "I am thinking about putting Mattie in charge. She's trained, knows the school, has multiple degrees, knows who's who, and she has a heart."

"She's amazing. Great choice." He didn't need her opinion. Drat.

"Your smile is beautiful, Gigi." He traced her knee with his free hand, and she desired to curl into him. "Next time you want to ask something, you can be direct. I don't bite."

"I like when you do," she whispered. "I wish there was more I could say."

"There is quite a lot you can say, but I will wait until we're alone without teenagers supervising our every action." He winked at her and sauntered off.

Her body shuddered on its own accord.

The hope of a future with Sean lay in her heart. Her skin heated from the pressure to let herself believe. She blinked and reminded herself she needed to prove she could be good for him, too.

Chapter 43

Gigi fought the tiredness on the drive but she hoped to get home and crawl into her bed. Finally she parked the car in her driveway and grabbed her bag. A minute later, she opened the door to her house and dropped her bags in a thud.

Now she wasn't tired. She yawned, and listed in her head her possible options on what to do next.

Tonight, Sean had gone home to his son.

She swallowed and told herself she'd see him tomorrow.

And the quietness of home helped her think.

She fixed her dinner, showered, and changed into a pair of sweats. Then she sat down with her newspaper and let her body sink into her couch.

A knock at the door interrupted her.

She found a bathrobe and rushed downstairs. Then she peeked out the door. Relief washed through her and she swung it open. "Mrs. Collins, I hadn't expected you."

"Margaret. You remember." The woman nodded at her but she held a few things tight in her arms.

"Margaret, yes. I didn't want to be rude." Gigi hesitated, unsure of what to say. "Can I help?"

"Let me in." Margaret held up her packages and shivered from the nip in the air. "We have a few things to talk about, dear."

Gigi stepped to the side and offered her home. "Does Sean know you're here?"

"No, and he doesn't know what we're going to talk about. I'm here about your mother. And it's something we should have talked about the day you moved back home." Margaret stepped inside, deposited the packages on the table near the door, and took off her jacket. "I became sidetracked but should have shown up sooner."

"My mother?" Intrigued, Gigi hung up the woman's coat on the hanger. "Would you like tea? Anything to drink?"

"I want to show you a few things I brought." Margaret clutched her packages again.

Gigi's eyes went to the notebook again. "What do you have there?"

"I should have come here the minute you moved home. Waiting this long had been wrong of me. I misplaced the notebook and planned on getting to this much sooner. Things in my life kept getting in the way, and in time, I hope you'll forgive me."

"Already done." Gigi directed her to sit on her couch and waited for Margaret to get comfortable. "Are you sure I can't get you anything? Is this because of Sean?"

"I'm here about your family, not mine." Shaking her head, Margaret asked, "Do you know your mother's name, Gigi?"

"Lillian Bradshaw Dumont Murphy. Oh wait, somehow the Patterson name before my name."

"No. Lillian was your stepmother. Your father married her weeks after you were born. Did she ever tell you, or did she enjoy torturing you to the day she died?" Margaret asked.

Gigi stared at her with her mouth open. "What did you just say, Margaret?"

"This has to be a shock. I forced the confession out of Lillian. Your mother, Amelie Dumont, was your father's first wife and your mother. She's from Quebec City, and she died in childbirth. Your dad was devastated, and Lillian pretended to want to be your mother for his money."

"Lillian thought money warmed her." Gigi blinked automatically. Her mind refused to process anything, and she sat in silence.

Margaret handed her the notebook.

Gigi accepted the paper, but blankly stared at it. "What is this?"

"Your father's journal. She gave it to me when I came here to find you," Margaret said. "Lillian must have known her façade kept cracking before his untimely death. She went too far with you."

Gigi stared at the paper, and memories floated in her head. "Lillian told me every day of my life I was her blood, and our family slept with rich men like your son."

"Don't repeat Lillian. My sons are Collinses. They will fall head over heels in love, never looking at another woman," Margaret said. "Lillian's dead and gone. You don't have to be afraid of her anymore."

"Margaret, I spent my life wanting to please her and never knowing how." Gigi shook her head firmly. "You taught me to survive. I learned how to cook, clean, and manage from you, the richest woman in town. Margaret, you were supposed to be eating bon-bons while servants took care of you."

"Eat too many bon-boons, and my husband won't be visiting my bed. I'd rather get my hands into something. Sitting around doing nothing sounds worse than death." Margaret paused, then asked, "Why are you sitting with blank papers around you, Geegs?"

Gigi's mind hadn't focused on the news yet. She couldn't. She spoke about what she understood. "My mother, I mean, Lillian, wanted your luxury and life. How do you know what you say or this notebook is real?"

"Gigi, I confronted Lillian when I learned what she did to you. Then when she sold you . . ." Margaret sighed. "Nothing happened to you then, but I had been too late to get to your house to get you out. I intended to move you into my house. We all know you had Sean's heart."

Tears formed in her eyes. Fear had forced her to run. Sean

and his entire family had looked out for her. "I left because I hadn't wanted her to tell you. I didn't want anyone to know."

Margaret snorted. "Lillian admitted everything that day, but she never did tell me where you went."

The words sank into Gigi's heart. Lillian hated her because she'd never be her. "Are you sure she was not my mother? This isn't a joke?"

"Your mother gave her life for you to be happy, Gigi. Giovanna was the name she chose." Margaret smiled. "Lillian was not sophisticated enough to choose a name like yours."

Gigi twirled off the couch and gazed out the window. The night sky and stars hadn't changed, but they now gave her a new focus. She stared up to find the patterns in the sky. For a few minutes, she said nothing. "The papers you asked about. I'm sitting here, alone, making a list of things I can do to win Sean's love. I stupidly thought no one should love me. Lillian convinced me I was worthless. Sean's been the only man in my heart, and I don't know how to help him."

Margaret stood up and brushed her hand on Gigi's arm. "Don't you know the best thing about Collins men?"

"What?"

"My boys and my husband's family, we fight hard for what we want. We're dead determined when our minds are made up. Conall stalked me until I admitted Daniel was his son, then he wouldn't take no for an answer. And I thought my no was final until he convinced me otherwise. Gigi, you're worse. And you're not Irish, so you don't have our stubbornness. You've been the woman in Sean's heart since you were practically still a baby. Your part of the relationship is to love and support him."

Gigi had no words. She'd never expected such a colossal change. Being free of her burdens sent a warmness through her body. "I'll want to read what my dad had to say."

"Of course, child," Margaret said. "Then I'll need you to

go to my son. He's cranky. Once you kiss and make up, I'll plan the wedding."

"We're not fighting. I kept my distance to think," Gigi answered. "It's only for tonight."

"Then come back to him after you finish reading," Margaret said then let her go to put on her jacket. "Moving Sean here is fine. We'll renovate this house to modernize everything, including the security."

Gigi stared after her, unsure what to say.

She'd dreamed to believe in a fairy tale. Sean had always starred as the handsome prince. But Lillian had tried to steal her happy-ever-after, and Gigi saw that now. She needed to sort this out then run to him. But first, she needed to read.

Chapter 44

Gigi woke up and went to work on empty. She had spent half the night reading. Her entire life had been a lie. Lillian's mantra to Gigi of never deserving love because she'd killed her father, then later on her baby, had all been lies.

Gigi understood now that she had never done anything to her father at age two, but Lillian repeating it so often had somehow forced guilt to sink into her skull and became a truth.

After work she needed to find Sean and apologize for her stupidity.

Love didn't require constantly proving oneself worthy. Love was both a give and take of acceptance. Gigi saw clearly now.

The coffee in her hand had done little to change her exhaustion. She assigned a project for the students to work on and finished her day.

Gigi cheered with the students at the announcement that Mattie was now principal.

Sean had kept his word. A true hero.

The bell rang, and students bounced out of her room and returned home. Gigi stretched. For the first time in years, her heart leapt for joy at the bell. She raced to her car.

She needed to find Sean.

A few minutes later, the gates to his parents' place opened. She parked her car in the visitors' section and knocked on the door. A young maid answered. She hadn't known her. "Is Sean in?"

"Mr. Collins is at work, Miss. Do you want to leave a message?"

Gigi had intended to pitch a tent at the front gate and wait for Sean. Instead, she asked, "Is Margaret here?"

The maid directed her into the lobby, held out her finger, and asked, "What's your name, Miss?"

"Gigi Dumont."

A moment later, Margaret called out on the speaker, "Gigi, I'm in the kitchen. Come in."

The house had newer decorations, but the Collinses hadn't changed much else. She wandered into the kitchen and saw Margaret mixing something in a bowl. "What are you making?"

"Finishing my batter for tomorrow's bread, then I'm about to start on adding seasonings to the chicken. Can you get the eggs and flour in two separate bowls for me?"

Washing her hands, Gigi remembered being in this kitchen many times before to help Margaret. She cleaned up the powder on the counter then found the bowls and the ingredients.

Margaret called out, "Sean will be home around six. Today was his first day in the office. How was your day, sweetie?"

Cracking an egg, Gigi blinked, then answered, "He doesn't know I'm here. Maybe I should go and come back later."

"Are you serious? You're staying put. Now wash your hands and start mixing the Italian spices."

Gigi grinned and followed orders. "Sean moved back in your home because he became sick. Has he talked about moving out?"

"You'll have to ask him, but I will tell you this. I want my boys living in the area. Gerard owns the house and acres of land on one side of the estate. He has an empty home, and we'll find him some woman to warm that place up. Daniel is looking at property nearby. Liam has threatened to move to New Zealand, but I'm working on him."

"And Sean?"

"Sean never moved far. With Jennifer, he stayed an hour north of here, but to me he moved much too far. He needs to be closer. Your house is the best location, but you'll need an upgrade to get rid of the stink of Lillian."

A young boy ran to the refrigerator, opened it up, and took out a cheese stick.

Margaret said, "Hey, now." She hugged the boy's shoulders and directed him to Gigi. "Say hi to my guest who's helping me cook dinner."

"Are you Gigi?" The boy's big blue eyes stared up at her.

"Yes." Gigi put the basil down. "We met once before. You're Patrick?"

"Good." The boy smiled. "You remembered me? Did Dad tell you about me?"

"He spoke about you every day in Paris. Do you mind me being here?"

Patrick shook his head no. "You're cooking with Grandma."

"Yep. First I help your grandma, and second, I plan to help make your dad have some fun," Gigi promised. "Can you help me?"

"Okay. Fun. I'm in." The boy turned to his grandmother. "Can I go now?"

Margaret let the boy go and soon footsteps echoed from the kitchen. Gigi retook her seat next to the basil. Then her hand shook and her heart thundered.

The boy rushed past her and knocked against her in his rush to squeal, "Dad!"

Almost dropping the basil, Gigi twirled around, heart pounding. "Sean, we weren't expecting you this soon."

"You don't answer your phone." He kissed her cheek. "Are you visiting my mom?"

"Yes," Margaret supplied. "She's helping me cook dinner. Go change. You can talk to Gigi after you've cleaned up."

"Mom, I'm an adult. This is a suit and tie."

Gigi laughed. Lightness settled into her heart. "Be happy you have a mom like Margaret, Sean."

"You're staying?" His gaze roamed her body then he met her eyes.

She nodded at him. "I'll finish helping."

"She's staying for dinner," Margaret said. "Gigi and I are talking real estate and business. Her house needs renovations. I won't let your girl here leave."

With a turn of her head, Margaret dismissed her almost thirty-year-old son.

Gigi walked beside her, then finished with the basil. "How in the world do you do it?"

"I promised you'd stay," Margaret told her. "Good. Now finish the preparations for the chicken spices. My son won't leave you alone soon enough."

Gigi followed her orders.

Patrick's excited booming voice recounted his adventurous day.

The smell of apples, lemon cleanser, and spices filled her nostrils, and reminded her of her younger years with Sean. Because he loved her, her childhood had not been horrible. In this house, she'd laughed.

Ten minutes later, the chicken went into the oven. Then Gigi stole away to the bathroom to fix herself up. Sean had looked handsome earlier.

Finished, she washed her hands. Then she left and stole away to the enclosed porch. The swings outside held lots of memories. She walked closer and decided to swing.

High in the air, again, she dreamt of flying. She'd wait for Sean, and not interrupt his reunion with his boy.

A giggle burst inside her. The wind rushed through her hair and she kicked higher and higher. Soon, she forgot everything else.

"You didn't have to wash up before dinner and I did?" Sean asked her in jest.

"Boys get dirtier."

"Says the girl with her feet in the sand."

She took in the sight of him and stopped kicking up in the swing. Blue jeans and a green T-shirt etched his hard body, and despite the breeze, her body heated up.

Stepping behind her, Sean pushed her back, and caused her to swing. His hands on her back created far more fireworks inside her. "Sean, I came over here to see you."

"No. Not yet, Gigi. Wait until Saturday."

She blinked rapidly.

"We're working on my schedule, and for once, you are going to follow my orders. I have plans for us."

"Your schedule includes us? Together?" she asked for assurance, but her heart knew the answer.

"Yes, and we do need to talk about everything, in private."

"Why Saturday?"

"Don't get ahead of me." He rocketed her back up, sounding affable. "We have a real date, just you and me. No teenagers, no mom, no children. Will you go?"

Biting her lip, she agreed. "Saturday, it is."

"Chin up, Geegs. It's in two days, and you have to work tomorrow. Be ready at ten A.M." He stopped her swing and held her with her ear next to his mouth. "I won't take no for an answer."

"I love you even more than I did when I was a girl. So yes to Saturday and everyday." She stepped off the swing and stared at him. He had wide grin on his face and his lips had parted. The warmth in his gaze sent a thrill inside her. "You're easy to love, handsome."

"Getting ahead of me again." Sean ran his hand through his hair. "Dinner's ready, Geegs. Let's go in."

Chapter 45

Gigi kicked her heels at work the next day. Waiting till Saturday would be entirely too long. Margaret texted her this morning that all her sons were flying into Boston today, and that Sean might be home late.

She'd like to see him every day. She'd tell him tomorrow, on his schedule, if she survived the next fourteen hours. She closed her eyes and sighed.

The bell at school rang, and students rushed home for a Friday. Erica and Kendra hedged in class. Gigi filed her paperwork, then asked, "Can I help you?"

Kendra smiled widely. "We have a gift certificate for you, Ms. Dumont. From the students from the trip. You have an appointment today after school."

"What if I'm busy?" Gigi had ethical issues about taking gifts. She didn't want to lose her job. "The thought is sweet."

Erica quoted, "School rules state you cannot accept a gift of over twenty dollars per student. This is a combined gift from us."

The rest of the students filed in. Raphael added, "We know you women want to look hot for men. Now go on."

Erica covered his mouth, telling him to shush.

Gigi smelled a plot. She opened the envelope and found a gift certificate and an appointment card for a prominent spa for her hair and a massage with body wrapping. "Did Mr. Collins tell you anything about me?"

"No, why?" Kendra's sweet smile smelled of a setup. "We all know he's your boyfriend now, because we locked you in the elevator."

"No. That wasn't right at all." Her face warmed and she feared a blush. Best to end the conversation. "Thanks. I'll get going then, or else I might miss the appointment."

The students looked congratulatory, but at least getting her hair done presented a distraction.

Her stomach refused to settle.

She left and took the appointment today.

Once at the fancy spa, her nose for a plot went up in droves. She had a four-hour spa appointment before her hair cut? Don't they close? And then the woman measured her waist and thighs 'for the body rub. "Did Sean Collins plan this?" Gigi asked her handler.

The woman shrugged. "Would you be upset if he had?"

Gigi must have made a face for the sales clerk said, "Relax and enjoy the spa."

A few hours later, Gigi came home, spray-tanned, hair cut, massaged, tweezed, and made over in a variety of manners. She called Sean on both his house phone and cellular, but he never answered.

She pressed her lips together and told herself it was one night. She'd survive till tomorrow and their big date. Now she needed to figure out what to wear. It was something to do. And if she didn't shake off her nerves, the date would have too much overloaded energy flying around. Staying calm, she trusted in love.

Chapter 46

A knock at the door came exactly as the clock indicated exactly ten A.M. Gigi applied the last layer of her lipstick, checked her jeans and shirt for strange stains, then opened the door.

Leaning on her door, Sean took her breath away in his black suit pants and crisp white shirt.

"Come in," she said. "I'm underdressed."

He brushed past her and handed her a single red rose. She took the flower to her nose then kissed him on the cheek. "I'll get a vase."

Arms snaked around her waist, preventing her from leaving. Slowly she turned back to him. Her skin brushed his body, and he warmed her. She kissed him on the lips. His firm, strong frame on her body flipped on a switch. She eased out of the kiss to say, "I love you. I've always loved you."

"Impossible, stubborn woman that you, Gigi. I love you, too. Now let's get going. We have a busy day."

Her body tingled. "What's going on? Let me go change into something nicer."

"Get your purse, Gigi. I have everything handled."

She followed directions. Then she rushed off to put the rose in water. Hurrying back, she grabbed her purse and took his hand, then locked the door behind her.

She glanced past his shoulder to the waiting limo. "We're going somewhere fancy? I do have nice dresses to wear."

"Get in the limo. Don't worry about where. Appease me, though, who do you love?"

"You." She laughed, kissed his cheek, and got in the limo.

When he closed the door behind him, she tickled him. He hadn't expected her to do that, laughed, and took her on top of him for a kiss. Then he tickled her stomach, causing her to flip back.

The limo took off. She pleaded, "Mercy, cheese head."

"What did you call me?" He kept tickling her.

"Che . . . ese . . . head." She giggled uncontrollably, but she squeaked out the word.

"Take it back." He continued tickling her unmercifully.

"Mercy, please Sean."

He stopped tickling her. "I can't believe you said that."

"You ate thirty pieces of cheese, proving something macho." She remembered one of the happy carefree days of childhood.

Sean brushed her hair with his hand. "Geegs, I've made some decisions regarding us."

She closed her eyes, letting the warmth envelop her and then laid her head on his shoulder. "Like what?"

"Like I need you to open your eyes."

A princess-cut two-carat diamond blinked at her, illuminating the darkness of the limo with bounces of color. Gigi blinked. "Is that what I think it is?"

"Marry me."

"What?" She lost her balance. "Are you serious?"

"I always pictured you when I heard the word 'wife.' The police closed their inquiry in Jennifer's death yesterday, ruling it death by natural cause, meaning my future is clear."

"Not what I meant." She sat up and put her hand on Sean's cheek. "You've been planning this day. How did you know I'd say yes?"

"Ahh." He laughed. "I couldn't imagine it any other way."

"Put the ring on me then."

The limo stopped and people partying could be heard outside.

Sean kissed her, and slipped the ring on at the same time.

She laughed. "I thought we were going to have the day to ourselves, alone."

"We will. Today is about us." He opened the door, and the crowd cheered, "Congratulations."

Sean helped her get out of the limo.

His four brothers were in suits. Then Gigi stared further into the crowd. Sean's parents were toasting with champagne, and a three-tier white cake sat on display in the gazebo. White chairs pointed in the distance, and a flowered aisle complete with a red walkway overlooked the bluff with the chapel. Realization took her a minute. "Did you plan our wedding?"

"My Gigi has this history of taking off on me, and I can't keep losing you. So our wedding is today."

Tears formed in her eyes. Happy tears. "Okay, Sean. You win this one time. I love you."

"Back at you, Geegs."

Also by Victoria Pinder and Soul Mate Publishing:

THE ZOASTRA AFFAIR

A hundred years from now, Earth has trading partners with alien beings, mostly humanoid. However, going into space has brought forth an unknown enemy who attacks Earth at will.

The Zoastra are part of the Earthseekers, an organization originally designed to go into space. Its new mission is to find Earth's enemies.

Ariel, stuck on a Victorian planet, steals Grace's body in order to get off the planet. Now Grace must get her body back before Ariel bonds with Grace's husband, Peter. Then there is Cross, the man on a mission to find those who killed his family. Ariel is attracted to Cross, but she's stolen someone's life. What can she do?

BORROWING THE DOCTOR

Daniel's tale, available summer 2014.

And,

ELECTING LOVE

Gerard's tale, available fall 2014

CPSIA information can be obtained
at www.ICGtesting.com
Printed in the USA
LVHW02s1320050718
582790LV00017B/361/P